JACQUELINE SUSANN'S
DOLORES

By Jacqueline Susann

DOLORES
ONCE IS NOT ENOUGH
THE LOVE MACHINE
VALLEY OF THE DOLLS
EVERY NIGHT, JOSEPHINE!

Jacqueline Susann's Dolores

William Morrow and Company, Inc.
New York   1976

Printed in the United States of America.

1 2 3 4 5   80 79 78 77 76

Library of Congress Cataloging in Publication Data

Susann, Jacqueline.
    Jacqueline Susann's Dolores.

    I. Title.
PZ4.S9596Do [PS3569.U75] 813'.5'4   76-3584
ISBN 0-688-03057-2

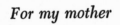

For my mother

Publisher's Note

This is Jacqueline Susann's last work. It was written in the autumn of 1973, and although she was then in the midst of her struggle with the cancer that would claim her life within the year, she was able not only to complete *Dolores* but also to revise it to her satisfaction.

Among the papers that were found after her death, there was a brief note in which she described the theme of the novel as "the most challenging and haunting on which I have ever worked."

Contents

PART ONE

1. Everything to Live For

THERE was a mean chill in the air as Air
Force One began its slow approach toward
Washington. Although the plane was warm,
the occupants could almost sense the dankness
below. Dolores shivered and folded her arms
about herself and stared at the lights below
. . . the thousands of tiny cars that moved like
an army of lemmings through the city. And
yet those rows of minuscule cars carried people
to visit friends . . . to a movie . . . to some
place they wanted to go. She shivered again
and huddled deeper in the seat. She was still
wearing the beige suit she had worn in New
Orleans.

It had been warm and sunny in New
Orleans. But it was winter in Washington. She
knew the press would be waiting for her when
she got off the plane. They were always waiting when she got off the plane . . . but this
would be the last time she would ever disem-

bark from Air Force One. James T. Ryan, affectionately called Jimmy by everyone, usually stretched out on the couch until the moment before landing (he still suffered pain from the broken vertebrae in his neck and the couch had been made especially for him) . . . only now he didn't feel any pain . . . and Elwood Jason Lyons was sitting on the couch. Jimmy was in the back . . . cold and alone . . . in a box with that bullet that hit him . . . clean and quick . . . right through his heart. They had caught the man immediately and riddled him with bullets as he tried to escape. H. Ronald Preston . . . a man with a greenish-white complexion . . . tall and thin . . . hawk-nosed. Why had he done it? Did he think that in his miserable little life, this one act would give him a permanent place in history? Was that worth dying for? Just to be remembered as the man who killed James T. Ryan. Maybe the H. Ronald Prestons of this world had nothing else to live for, and dying spectacularly was the only important thing they could do. But Jimmy had everything to live for . . . God, no one loved life as much as Jimmy. Just this morning . . . the pride on his face as the audience called out "DOLORES!" . . . "DOLORES!" And the lovely little Italian woman who had given her a flower and murmured, "*Multibella!*" She certainly didn't look *multibella* now. One of her white gloves was missing and there was blood all over the suit.

Jim liked the suit . . . it didn't look as expensive as it really was. Oh God, why had she argued with him all that weekend about the luggage and the clothes she took? She had wanted to look her best, and had brought several changes even though Betsy Minton had checked and rechecked the weather reports . . . one could never tell. Right now, Betsy was with the children. Thank God for Betsy. She had started as a housekeeper when Jim was just a Senator . . . and when he had become President, she had elevated Betsy to personal maid and secretary. Betsy did everything. She had even taken the children to Jim's sister —and when the proper moment came, Betsy would break it to them.

Break what to them? That their father had been shot while he was being cheered at a speech . . . that they would have to leave the White House . . . that their entire world had changed. Would they understand about death? Mary Lou was six. She had seen her doggy die. She understood about Heaven. But the twins . . . little Jimmy and Mike . . . they were only three . . . they still couldn't differentiate between God and Santa Claus. She hadn't even tried to explain Jesus. Just last night in New Orleans, she and Jim had discussed religion. Was it *just last* night? He had wanted to go to bed with her but she was expecting the hairdresser at eight in the morning and there was the breakfast ceremony and then the long ride through the city to the huge auditorium where he was to make the speech. It was hot in New Orleans and her hair really had to be done. Jim had smiled . . . he understood. Part of the duties of being First Lady was to look perfect. She sure didn't look perfect now . . . the wrinkled suit . . . her hair falling across her face . . . and now she'd never be able to go to bed with Jim again . . . never! *No* . . . she mustn't allow the tears to come. A lady doesn't show emotion in public.

2. First Lady

SHE felt a gentle hand pat her on the arm. Who dared to touch her! She was Dolores Ryan, First Lady . . . Oh God, no, she was Dolores Ryan, private citizen now . . . and the gentle hand that patted her arm belonged to Elwood Jason Lyons, the *new* President of the United States. He managed a sympathetic smile as he walked on down the aisle. She stared at the skinny back of the new President. She watched him sit beside his buxom wife— the new First Lady. They would live in her beloved White House, the place she had redecorated and made so beautiful. The place where she wanted Mike, Jimmy and Mary Lou to spend eight wonderful years. Elwood and Lillian's children would live there now. Ellie, Edie, Elwood, Jr., and Edward. Nice enough children but they wouldn't appreciate the beauty she had brought into the White House. She couldn't picture Lillian Lyons living in her white and yellow bedroom. Or one of the girls living in Mary Lou's bedroom. All yellow and white, a miniature version of "Mommy's." No, they'd change all that . . . and Elwood would probably change Jimmy's room. Elwood Jason Lyons thought of himself as a man of the people. He never let anyone forget his grandfather had been a coal miner. And that he liked plain ordinary food. They'd probably have wienie roasts right on the White House lawn. Oh Lord, why was she thinking in such *non-sequiturs*. Jimmy wouldn't like her to put down the Lyonses. Besides, there was nothing wrong with hot dogs. Jimmy loved them. When they went on the family's beach parties at Newport Beach, the whole clan ate hot dogs and Jimmy's brother, Michael, even used to put on a chef's hat when he served. The Ryans adored hot dogs and corn on the cob. Jimmy used to get so angry when she packed a picnic basket of paté and cucumber sandwiches for herself. And he grimaced at the thin watercress sandwiches she often served for tea. He also thought her passion for caviar was ridiculous.

Caviar! That brought back memories of Paris. Paris had given them some wonderful close moments. There weren't too many of those moments in their lives . . . and, oddly enough, most of them came out of tragedy. Like now, she felt Jimmy was not cold and dead in that flag-draped box. He belonged to her. But he didn't belong to her. Impersonal doctors' hands would touch him and cut him open and do an autopsy and . . . Oh God, he hated illness or weakness . . . he had been thrown from a horse a year after their marriage and his collarbone had been broken. And how he had hated all those weeks in traction in the hospital, with nurses handling him, doctors probing, and no noticeable signs or promises of complete recovery. He had been so brave . . . until that one day when she saw the lone tear travel down his cheek. She had kissed it off with her lips and held his hand . . . and he had managed a weak smile. Why had she been able to show her feelings then (was it because of *his* vulnerability?)? He always seemed a bit aloof when he was strong. But in the hospital for just one precious moment he had reached out for her emotionally. He had never done that before. Even on their honeymoon, he had wanted her . . . taken her . . . but had not seemed to belong to her in any way. There had always been a part of James T. Ryan that he kept to himself, a strange coolness that would occasionally come to his eyes, a look that said, "No trespassing." Oddly enough, she had always run into this obstacle with anyone she loved or cared about. Her tennis pro when she was fifteen . . . she hadn't an inkling he was a homosexual . . . and the times he had walked off the court with his arm loosely draped around her had been enough to give her hours of schoolgirl dreams. But the dreams

had lasted only a few precious weeks. Then
her mother had dropped the bomb. When she
caught Dolores staring at Billy, she laughingly
explained to Dolores that Billy had a friend, a
special friend named Bob.

She had continued to adore the tennis
lessons, but had held back her emotions because she knew Billy had a world of his own
. . . a world she could not enter.

Like Jimmy's private world . . . Jimmy
had recovered . . . there had never been a
hint of a tear again. He was the old Jimmy
. . . invincible . . . "Superman." And then
one night she saw the bottles in his medicine
chest. All marked "For Pain." And when she
watched closely she saw a tightness in his jaw
at times . . . a pill popped into his mouth
when he thought no one was looking . . . and
suddenly she was aware of the daily massages,
the steam baths, the therapist who came to
give him special exercises. But no admission of
pain on his part, no close moments until the
night of the debacle of the River War in South-
east Asia when so many American soldiers were
killed. He had come to her bedroom that night
to tell her the news. She had never seen him
so defeated . . . and she had sprung into his
arms because she had seen the tears in his eyes.
And that night in bed they had clung together
. . . not even a night on their honeymoon had
they ever been so close. She was sure the
second set of twins was conceived then. And

she carried her large belly with pride, because these two babies had come from moments of their deepest love.

She hadn't been able to take it when they were stillborn. Little Timothy and William. There had been a hint of tears in Jimmy's eyes too, but he had held them back because she was sobbing so hard. That's when he had said, "Dolo . . . I've always felt God has singled me out for some kind of greatness . . . and they say that with greatness goes tragedy. And remember, it's you who have to share both the greatness and the tragedy. So, remember, a Ryan never shows weakness in public. If you don't win the game in tennis, you jump over the net as if you had like a champion and congratulate the opponent." And then through her sobbing she had shouted, "But I'm not a Ryan . . . I'm a Cortez . . . I'm of Castilian descent . . . Latins are emotional." And she had wanted to cry out, "And Latins want to show their feelings . . . share feelings . . . be close . . . not just at certain times."

Yes, the closeness came during the tragedies.

3. Nita

AND now this was the biggest tragedy of all. "Jimmy," she whispered to herself, "I can't hold you in my arms because you're back there . . . growing colder every moment in that box. That's why I put my St. Theresa necklace around your neck. My father put it on me when I was seven. I never took it off. At least with that medal we are together. I hope there really is a hereafter because there were so many times we were apart . . . so many times I found it impossible to tell you how I felt . . . but I'll try to do what you would want me to do today . . . I'll be a Ryan. And I won't cry . . . I didn't cry when I stood next to Elwood and heard him sworn in. I pretended I was a real Ryan. Oh Jimmy, I promise! No one will ever forget that I am Dolores Ryan . . . and no one will ever forget you. I'll see to that. Jimmy, is there really anything . . . after . . . can you see into my mind . . . are

you 'up there' . . . have you met my father?
They used to call him Dashing Dan because he
was so handsome. He loved beautiful women,
too . . . that's why my mother left him. But
she was wrong because she sort of dried up
after that. And no man could replace him and
she would watch him dating all those beautiful
actresses and models in New York. That's why
I never left you, Jimmy. All those times when
you—but I won't think of it now. You belong
to me now . . . forever . . . and I'll try to
make you proud of me. The way you were that
time in Paris . . . when you finally admitted
that caviar didn't really taste bad at all."

Caviar . . . there had been tons of
caviar in Paris. That was when she had come
into her own. Until Paris she had always been
the blue blood, the pretty girl-woman married
to a man with movie star looks and unbelievable charisma. She had been the unknown
entity . . . a girl from a fine family . . . but
a blank. And then that trip to Paris, during his
second year of the Presidency. The French had
adored her. They had admired her chic clothes
and her easy fluency with the language. Poor
Jimmy, he had sputtered a well-rehearsed
greeting, but it had been Dolores who had
taken over Paris. That was the first time she
had seen the new look in Jimmy's eyes. Actually it was not really a new look . . . it was
the *old* look . . . the look he had given her
when they were first dating . . . the look he

had given her when she wore all those beautiful dresses on their honeymoon. The look that had vanished after the birth of Mary Lou. The look that had been replaced with guilt because he knew she had learned about Tanya. During the last months of her pregnancy, all of her "best friends" had hinted about Tanya. Elegant Tanya with the slight accent, married to an elderly Senator. Jimmy had disappeared a lot during those last months, while she sat with the heaviness ill-concealed even in chic made-to-order pregnancy clothes. He always had an excuse . . . some official business . . . a meeting with his brother . . . but it hadn't taken her long to learn about his unofficial visits to the lovely house in Georgetown . . . especially when the elderly Senator was on his estate in Maryland. The Senator was twenty years older than Tanya and he knew all about the romance, but how could he compete with any man who wanted the beautiful Tanya, especially when the man was the President of the United States?

But Paris had changed things. Dolores had come into her own as a full-fledged glamorous personality. And it had been like a second honeymoon. Even Jimmy's attitude about sex had been more intimate than aggressive. Sometimes it bothered Dolores. She had never been able to abandon herself in sex. In fact, she had to grit her teeth each time she allowed Jimmy to make love to her. She had pretended to feel a climax to build up his ego . . . and it wasn't until Jimmy stopped asking that she found herself wanting it. Not wanting it out of desire . . . but wanting it because it gave her the security of her own femininity to know she was desired. Sometimes she read the movie magazines where she was called beautiful. Secretly she cut out the pictures of herself on the covers . . . and would stare in the mirror and whisper, "I *am* beautiful." Actually, she didn't believe it. Nita was the beauty. Juanita and Dolores Cortez . . . eleven months apart . . . the most beautiful debutantes in New York. How she had envied Nita's looks . . . *and* Nita was only five foot four . . . never too tall for a man. Dolores was five foot seven . . . marvelous now for fashion . . . marvelous because Jimmy had been six foot one. But at sixteen she had always felt oafish and clumsy around Nita.

And all those secret tears she had swallowed when Nita became engaged to Lord Bramley. Dolores had adored Lord Nelson Bramley. And she had felt he admired her. They had met at "their" coming-out party, a party when she and Nita had been presented together. Being "presented" at nineteen! But it was the only way her mother had been able to manage it, presenting the two sisters together. Things had been rough after her father's death. The Cortezes were still high in the Social Register but nil in Dun and Bradstreet. But with it all, the debut of Dolores and Juanita had been an important social event. Every eligible male had accepted. With the help of an old friend who had turned society press agent, Mrs. Cortez had even managed to have a few titles attend. Lord Nelson Bramley was the outstanding name. Not only was his lineage perfect, he was also a millionaire . . . and he was the most handsome man Dolores had ever seen.

Lord Bramley had danced with Nita a few times but it had been Dolores he had danced with most of the evening. After that, he had taken them both to the theater several times. And then there was the night he came to call . . . to speak to Mrs. Cortez alone. Dolores waited in her bedroom, trying to hide her excitement, while Nita placidly played solitaire on the bed. It seemed an eternity before Mrs. Cortez sent for both girls. She was smiling happily. Lord Bramley had asked for *Nita's* hand. Somehow Dolores had managed a bright smile as her mother beamed and Nita demurely accepted.

Yes, in the beginning, Nita had it all. Tiny . . . slim figure . . . heavy black hair. (Dolores had been born with mousy brown hair and had started streaking it with peroxide at school . . . she felt she had to when people kept commenting on Nita's striking coloring.) Nita's marriage had been spectacular. For weeks, the newspapers carried pictures of Nita

and Lord Bramley. The Beautiful Pair . . .
dining at the Colony . . . lunching at "21."
Often Dolores was included in the luncheons
. . . she tried to decline but she knew she had
to make some appearances. At night, alone in
bed, she refused to allow herself to cry, because
she felt if she ever let loose, she would have
no control.

　　She managed to go to Nita's fittings for
her trousseau and wedding gown (the last of
the Georgian silver and Limoges china had
been sold for these luxuries). "Dolo," her
mother had said, "you're just going to have to
elope when your big moment comes! I can't
afford another wedding." Dolores had gotten a
job with the U.N. as a translator. She had not
only conquered French but was fluent in Spanish and she began to study Russian—anything
to obliterate Nita's marriage and all the attending press.

4. The Baron

SHE had been at the U.N. a year when she met James T. Ryan. She realized he was marvelously attractive but she was unable to feel any emotion about him. It was too soon after Lord Bramley. However, they dated whenever he was in New York and she pretended an enthusiasm she didn't feel. After all, dating *the* most eligible attractive Senator was a coup . . . and when their pictures began to appear in the society columns, she promptly sent them to Nita.

She knew it didn't impress Nita. Nita still had it all. She had had two lovely sons within three short years after her marriage. Her pictures appeared in *Women's Wear* attending every lavish European ball. She commuted between London, Paris, and Italy, and Dolores was quick to note that Nita had at least seven fur coats.

But it didn't hurt as much because Nita

was in London . . . and she was in New York in the thick of it, with a dashing Senator commuting to see her. James T. Ryan was the direct opposite of Lord Nelson Bramley. His father, Timothy Ryan, never hid the fact that he had worked as a bricklayer in Shamokin, Pennsylvania . . . came to Philadelphia with eight hundred dollars and wound up becoming the top contractor in the East. He owned property and buildings in Philadelphia, New York, Boston, Detroit, Chicago. He bought up real estate in Florida in the thirties when it was cheap . . . he became a multimillionaire before his two sons and three daughters were in their teens. Yet he always remained "one of the people." His wife, Bridget, was beautiful and strong. She shut her eyes to his notorious affair with a famous sculptress and went to Mass twice a day and prayed for strength. And when he had his first major heart attack, he gave up the sculptress and came home to Bridget.

Dolores had gone with Jimmy almost a year when Nita arrived with the children and Lord Bramley for a Christmas visit. She had two nurses and was buried deep in sable when Dolores and her mother met them at the airport. Lord Bramley had borrowed a friend's plane, and Nita and the Lord were whisked through Customs. Once again Dolores felt oversized and unattractive. The next day they had a quiet chat over a private luncheon at Orsini's (while the newspapermen and cameramen were waiting outside for Nita) and Dolores was conscious that every woman in the room was staring at Nita's twenty-carat diamond and her new mink sport coat. She tried to conceal the envy that was welling up inside of her. She had thought it was gone. She made proper small talk and tried to like Nita as she watched her sister light up one cigarette after another. It wasn't until after the espresso was served that Nita leaned over and whispered, "Dolo, I'm pregnant again."

"How marvelous. This time it will be a girl."

"I haven't told Nelson."

"Why not?"

"Because I want to get rid of it. You must know places . . . or the proper doctor."

Dolores stared at her sister. "How would I know?"

"Well, Dolo . . . you're almost twenty-two . . . you must have had a few accidents. Personally, I'm afraid of the 'ring' . . . and the diaphragm never seems to work with me. Dolo, you've got to help me."

Dolores had stared at her napkin. She was ashamed to admit she had no concern about a diaphragm . . . or a ring (she didn't even know what the ring was). She had been dating Jimmy in the most casual way for a year. It had been her work that occupied her time. She had mastered Russian and was now studying Greek. She was silent for a moment and then said quietly, "I don't know of any such doctors . . . and besides, why should you want to get rid of it? You know that's a mortal sin."

"Oh Lord, don't tell me you're still steeped in the Church."

"Not steeped . . . but I believe in it and go to Mass every Sunday. We were raised as Catholics . . . I'm not strict and I must admit it's been ages since I've gone to confession . . . but I couldn't knowingly commit a mortal sin."

"Well, dammit . . . I can't be saddled down with more than two children . . . I've got to be free."

"What about Nelson?"

Nita laughed. "Oh Dolo . . . he had a mistress when we got married. Everyone in Europe knew about it except me. But he needed the proper wife . . . and it seems he studied me as if I were a horse for breeding. He came right out and told me, after the honeymoon. He even told me the name of his mistress . . . Angelina . . . an Italian-Swiss girl. She's a journalist . . . and he's set her up in Paris and spends every weekend with her."

Dolores reached out and pressed her sister's hand. "Oh Nita, I'm so sorry."

"Don't be," Nita snapped. "And don't look sorry for me. Half the room is staring at us. I am Lady Bramley . . . and he is very generous. Of course, the jewelry belongs in the

family . . . but I've got everything . . . a
beautiful flat in Belgravia . . . thirty rooms
and seven in help . . . a huge country place
. . . almost palatial. He's not the richest man
in Europe . . . I mean we don't have yachts or
a string of horses . . . but we are rich. And
he is Catholic, so divorce is out. But I'm not
going to be like Mother . . . I told him we'd
put up a marvelous front . . . but I intend
to have my affairs too. That's why I've got to
get rid of this child."

Nita had found a "proper doctor" on her
own and rid herself of the child. Then she returned to London and once again began ap-
pearing in *Vogue* and *Women's Wear* and all
the European magazines with Nelson smiling
at her side. But in her quick notes to Dolores,
she hinted at a brief love affair with an Italian
movie star . . . a swift and tumultuous romance with a croupier in a London gambling
club . . . and was currently swooning over
Baron Erick de Savonne, one of the richest men
in the world. Dolores couldn't understand this
current affair. She had met the Baron once
when she went to London to visit Nita. It had
become a familiar pattern . . . she always
dashed off to London when Jimmy had a new
"girl." The papers always wrote it up as a
"visit" to her sister, followed with paragraphs
on how close the sisters were. (Jimmy never
made any permanent liaison . . . not after
Tanya, and when Dolores would take off he

always broke with the girl of the moment and bombarded Dolores with pleas to return.) On one of these visits Dolores had met the Baron briefly. He had "accidentally" run into them at Mirabelle (this time the reporters outside were waiting for Dolores. She wasn't just another English title . . . she was the wife of the President of the United States).

5. The Most Beautiful Woman in the World

THE Baron had joined them for a coffee. He had a scar over one eye, "a saber scar" he had told them. In reality, he had gotten it when he single-handedly broke up a dock strike. He owned a larger fleet of tankers than Onassis . . . he had vast holdings in the Near and Middle East. Baron Erick de Savonne was built like a prizefighter and was known to have been in many a brawl on the docks. Yet he also owned many luxury hotels throughout the world and an art collection worth billions.

He lived lavishly and kept a ballerina who was past her prime for many years. She was inscrutably beautiful, but it didn't seem to bother Nita. "I have to give some of my time to Nelson . . . and go to certain social affairs . . . and I'd rather know Erick was with a woman he'd had for years than flirting with someone else. When the times comes, I'll marry him."

In the beginning, Dolores had been

shocked at the idea of divorce. But Nita made
no bones about her break with the Church.
And gradually Dolores had shrugged it off.
After all, it was Nita's life. Her own life now
seemed far more glamorous. She was on movie
magazine covers . . . on *Life* . . . *Look* . . .
Time . . . *Newsweek* . . . and when Nita
came to visit her, Nita was now the sister of
the First Lady . . . sister of the most beautiful woman in the world.

Most beautiful woman in the world!

Dolores adored that title. She wasn't
tiny or pencil-thin like a model. She weighed
one hundred and twenty-five . . . but Donald
Brooks designed clothes for her that made her
appear regal and slim. Her hair was augmented
with hairpieces and she wore it like a lion's
mane. Her posture was perfect and she kept a
perpetual tan and managed to stride into a
room with a walk that was all her own. Part
panther . . . part athlete. And beside her, Nita
now looked small and unimportant.

But Nita rarely came to the States, and
with her own fame on the rise, Dolores grew
closer to her sister. There was no one else she
could really trust. It hadn't all been beautiful
and romantic with Jimmy. Their marriage had
been recorded in the society columns because
of the Cortez name and the Ryan millions. And
in all the interviews it bothered her because
Old Man Ryan—Timothy Ryan—never let anyone forget his humble beginnings. Bridget had

not come from a humble background. Her
family were upper-middle-class Irish Catholic
and her father had been a respected lawyer in
Cleveland. But she subjected herself to Timothy's bombastic tirades about the American
Dream . . . that he had started as a bricklayer, yet his son might one day be President
of the United States. No one took the "President" part seriously. Least of all Jimmy. His
father had poured money into his campaign to
get him and his brother, Michael, their Senate
seats, and both Jimmy and Michael were quite
content to stay there.

And this was the family Dolores had
married into. Their great wealth was the intri-
cate lure. She liked Jimmy, but socially it had
been a big step down. Nita had sent her money
for a trousseau and a wedding. When Dolores
tried to refuse, Nita said, "Darling, I'm crawl-
ing with money . . . from my husband . . .
and from the Baron. Ten thousand is just
pocket money."

It had been a lovely wedding and
Jimmy had taken her on a quiet European
honeymoon. It had been fun wearing her new
pretty clothes. She and her mother had really
bargain-hunted in New York. But she knew
after the marriage that all would be different.
When she was Mrs. James T. Ryan, she'd
have all the money she needed. And she'd pay
back Nita.

During their honeymoon abroad, Nita

had entertained them. Everyone had liked
Jimmy. It was after the honeymoon that the
disappointing realities set in. She had stared in
horror at the small house in Georgetown that
Jimmy had bought without consulting her. She
hid her unhappiness as he carried her over the
threshold with pride. And there were Bridget
and Timothy and Michael and his wife, Joyce,
and the three sisters all squealing and hugging
her. And through it all she saw the ordinary furniture . . . the imitation Queen Anne chairs.
And there was Betsy Minton . . . his housekeeper . . . eager to "do" for her.

Dolores couldn't believe it. Timothy
Ryan's worth was often estimated at forty million . . . and Jim, his brother and sisters were
the sole heirs. She had expected Jimmy to give
her a free hand, to pick a house of her own
choosing, decorate it, hire a staff of servants,
give brilliant dinner parties. But instead she
found he was almost penurious. "Dolo, we have
a huge estate in Virginia. It's the family place
and we all go there for weekends. There's also
a family place in Newport . . . large enough
for the whole brood . . . so anytime you want
sun, it's there waiting. And when you want
the country, it's also there."

"But it's not mine . . . ours."

"It is ours," he said firmly. "The family's.
We love the country place. In the summer, we
love to water ski, to swim . . . and you'll fit
in just great. I picked the house in Georgetown

because it has four bedrooms . . . enough for us and three or four children . . . even five if we double them up. I've got a lot of studying to do . . . this job in the Senate is way over my head. I'm not a political animal. I'd much rather have stayed with law."

"Then why didn't you?"

He had looked sheepish. "Dad has this crazy idea of me being President."

"Why doesn't he groom Michael for it? He's a Senator, too. And he's three years older than you."

"Michael had too tough a time passing law. He's even less of a politician than I. He's been married to Joyce for only six years and they have five kids and another on the way. He's a stay-at-homer . . . so the load fell on me."

Their first real argument came when she bought ten pairs of shoes. Jimmy had stared at the bill with total disbelief. "How can you wear ten pairs of shoes at once?"

"They match different clothes—clothes I intend to buy."

"We've been married only two months, Dolo."

"Meaning what?"

"Meaning a bride's trousseau should last at least a year. My mother bragged that hers lasted five years. Of course, she was in maternity clothes a lot . . . and you probably will be, too. So don't go on any buying sprees."

It was almost too much for her to cope with. Obviously he had learned the value of a hard-earned dollar from his father. His mother cared little for clothes. She still played tennis every day, wore slacks, and her figure was firm and slim enough to pass for a girl's. Even now, at seventy-two, she took pride in her activities . . . her charities. Dolores was a complete sybarite. Her father had told her that when she was very young. If he offered to buy her a lollipop, she wanted one in every color. Sometimes she never ate them . . . but she liked to know they were there. She had adored her father. That had been the first wrench . . . when he left her mother and she read about him with all those beautiful women. Nita took it all philosophically. "We were bound to lose him one day . . . when we go off to our own husbands." But whenever Dolores saw her father, he always indulged her . . . tea at the Plaza . . . pretty dresses from an expensive place on Madison Avenue . . . and he never remarked as all the salesgirls did how much easier Nita was to fit than Dolores.

6. *Secret Service*

AND even after the marriage when Mary Lou and the twins were born . . . and the fantastic whirlwind of the Presidential nomination and election . . . he had still kept after her about the bills. Just a month ago he had sent Betsy Minton, now elevated to her personal secretary, to give her instructions that she must "cut down." Finally, after a heated battle he blurted out, "Dolo, we don't have all that money. My father always exaggerated our fortune. We are worth perhaps three or four million dollars in cash. Of course, that doesn't include our real estate holdings. And don't forget . . . my election cost a fortune. Of course, there are trusts set aside for the children . . . and a trust of a million that we'll inherit when I'm sixty . . . by that time we can both relax and enjoy life. But for the present, we must take things easy."

And when Nita came to town and

bought two dozen pairs of shoes, or three fur coats from Maximilian, Dolores merely smiled and said it didn't fit her image as First Lady. But oh God, how she longed to own all those beautiful furs and clothes. But she consoled herself with the fact that Nita was just *her* sister now. *She* was Dolores Ryan . . . and even Nita began to feel it. One night when they were going to the opening of an art show for charity, Nita said, "With all my jewels, Dolo . . . it will be you who will be photographed." And it had been true.

They went to Orsini's and she sat back and allowed Nita to pick up all their luncheon checks. Nita wasn't married to a "broke" millionaire. Nita also received insane gifts from the Baron, who was now becoming an obsession with her. She had tried every lure but he was not talking marriage. Yet despite Nita's money, Nita seemed to trail behind her. Her camellia-like daintiness now looked vapid. Dolores was the trend setter . . . the lioness . . . who covered all the pages of *Vogue* and *Harper's Bazaar*. Dolores, who could "make" a designer if she "accepted" or wore his new creation. Dolores, the first lady of fashion. Dolores, the First Lady of the land!

Only she wasn't First Lady anymore. She was a widow and Lillian Lyons, in her beat-up Persian lamb coat, was First Lady. She stared over at the new "First Couple."

Lillian, middle-aged, tall, a big woman . . . and Elwood, short and skinny. All the glamour she and Jimmy had given to the White House would vanish . . . and she would vanish with it. Suddenly she sat up straight. No, she wouldn't vanish. In the beginning, she had walked in Jimmy's shadow, came into her own after Paris, ignored the gossip about him with Hollywood stars, because deep down she couldn't blame him. She wasn't exactly a ball of fire in his arms . . . maybe it had been the nagging poverty and pretense of good living after her father's death; her mother's constant jibing . . . "If I hadn't been so insanely in love with your father, I could have married into great wealth." Yet when her mother died, she had mumbled . . . "I'm coming, Dannie!" Even in death, her mother had reached out for her father's arms. And it was then that she had remembered the tears her mother shed when her father had stayed out on his "poker" nights . . . and the tears when he wouldn't take her on "business trips" . . . and the times when her mother had sobbed and said to the ten-year-old Dolores, "Oh Dolo, never fall in love. Once you do you never belong to yourself . . . you're just a slave . . . half a person without him."

She had never "belonged" to Jimmy. She had flirted when they met because he was so handsome. Her mother had thought he was common-looking . . . but her mother had approved of the Ryan money . . . and thank God, it was there, because the cancer hit her mother two months after the wedding and it was the Ryan money that made the last six months of her life painless.

Dolores had not gone to bed with Jimmy until they were married. If he was surprised to find her a virgin he said nothing. But from the very beginning sex was something she had submitted to. She liked being his wife . . . adored being First Lady . . . learned to grow accustomed to unlimited servants, Secret Service men . . . limousines . . . world acclaim . . . and finally open envy in Nita's eyes. Yet one bullet from an H. Ronald Preston . . . and all that was gone . . . and she'd probably go back to being the less attractive sister.

No! She might not be the President's wife anymore, but she would hold on to her newly acquired fame. She loved seeing herself in the newspapers, she loved the crowds that followed her and the Secret Service men in attendance. Well, as Elwood had explained, she would still be entitled to Secret Service men for herself and the children.

7. The Reigning Queen

SHE knew the plane was circling for a landing. She had to get her thoughts together. She would keep Betsy Minton on. She wondered what would happen to the trust fund. Jimmy was only forty-two. They had never discussed wills . . . they were both so young and healthy.

But there had to be plenty of money. And the important thing was to keep her celebrity status alive. One of the aides was saying something. She listened again.

"Mrs. Ryan, I've laid out a navy blue suit, and some white gloves. You can change in the bedroom area in the back of the plane. And you might want some help with your hair. One of the girls, Beatrice, says she can get it into a neat French twist like Dino sometimes does . . ."

"No," Dolores said quietly. "I want the

press to see the blood of my husband . . . the blood he shed for his country."

"Oh, Mrs. Ryan, you can't," the aide said.

"I can . . . and I will!"

And then she stood at the ramp, a rumpled tigress with a wide-eyed lost little girl look. The cameras flashed, the newsreels ground, and she stood there dry-eyed. Not the shy young First Lady, but an angry panther bringing her slain mate to rest. Michael, Jimmy's brother, was waiting to escort her through the crowd.

Elwood Jason Lyons and Mrs. Lyons followed her at a discreet distance. Mrs. Lyons was furious. Her husband was the President. He had been sworn in on the plane. Why was he walking behind this young girl, as if she was still the reigning Queen? And the press . . . they were taking more pictures of her and Michael than they were of the new First Lady and President. Look at the way Michael was taking over. He had never been close to Dolores, but now he was acting like the heir apparent. His wife hadn't even come with him . . . he had his arm around Dolores. Good Lord, was he thinking of becoming the next President? His absentee record in the Senate was a joke. But these days anything was possible. He was even better-looking than Jimmy . . . the whole damn family was so good-looking. All the cameramen were following the Ryans . . . of course, they had taken pictures of Elwood and she had tried to slouch as she stood beside him . . . why did she have to be three inches taller than Elwood! Well, she'd buy lower heels . . . and she'd make Elwood get those lifts.

But the press was all with Dolores and Michael now, and the official White House car was taking *them* to the White House. She turned to Elwood. "How long does she stay?"

"Honey." Elwood's soft voice was gentle. "Her husband isn't even in the ground yet. Then there's the funeral . . . and we have to give her time to find a place to live."

"Well, my children are going to get newspaper space from now on," Lillian said. "I'm sick of reading about little Jimmy and Mike and Mary Lou."

"The children are nice kids," Elwood said. "It's the newspapers that have doted on them . . . calling them pet names. You know the President's wife wants to be called Dolores, not Dolo."

"*I'm* the President's wife," she hissed. "Even you . . . you still regard that snooty blonde as the First Lady." Then she forced a smile as a cameraman dropped away from the crowd following Dolores and snapped her.

Dolores walked with Michael and fought the uncontrollable urge to sob. The protective arm of Jimmy's brother only made her realize how alone she really was. Michael didn't give a damn about her . . . he had always thought her a snob . . . but he was acting in the true Ryan fashion. The family stays together. And Michael was sticking to the rules.

"I've talked to the Cardinal. We'll plan the funeral with him tomorrow," Michael whispered. "You go home and get a good night's sleep. Betsy Minton brought the kids to us. Joyce has them all comfy and playing with our brood. They don't understand, any of them, quite what happened. Even our ten-year-old doesn't understand death. But she's acting like a little mother already to your kids. Now about the funeral . . . I figured on a private High Mass . . . and private interment. Jimmy served in the Army but I figure we can bypass Arlington and bury him in our family plot in Virginia. It will save you a lot of wear and tear. Bridget will handle things . . ."

"That's very kind of you," she said softly. "And I admire the way the Ryans all stick together. But Jimmy was *my* husband."

"Well, sure . . . anything you say."

"I want to know how President Kennedy was buried!"

PART TWO

8. Thirty-six

DOLORES stared at the gray East River. Then she walked from the den into the massive living room. How would she pass another day? It was almost a year since Jimmy had been assassinated. A year, during which Dolores was not supposed to "go out." Oh, an occasional lunch with the "right" person was permissible. It broke in every newspaper and caused talk for days. But right now she was lonely. Damned lonely.

She had gone to London after the funeral services. They had been impressive and correct. She and Michael had sat up all night and read every press clipping about Jack Kennedy's funeral, about Lincoln's funeral—and they had done it all. Only she hadn't been able to take the twins. She managed to make Mary Lou stand still through it all, but it had been rough. Then she had taken the children and Betsy Minton to London to stay with Nita.

Nita had been furious that she couldn't give parties for Dolores. "It's ridiculous for you to play the bereaved widow. He cheated on you all the time . . . everyone knows that . . . I mean, he wasn't anything like his brother, who is one of the last of the living 'family' men."

"But Nita . . . toward the end . . . I did love Jimmy."

Nita had stared at her defiantly. "Dolo, you love only one person—yourself. And keep it that way. Here I am, actually carrying a torch for Erick—"

"Erick?"

"The Baron."

Dolores laughed. "You're torching for his money. Not him."

"I have enough money," Nita said.

"Then why?" Dolores asked. "He's gross . . . he's ugly."

"Maybe it's Erick's power that fascinates me. You know there were women who were fascinated with Hitler and Mussolini just because of their power."

"You make a great case for both yourself and Erick."

"Well, his power *is* part of it," Nita said. "But last night, when he dropped by—didn't you feel he had a certain magnetism?"

"I felt nothing . . . and I'm sure that through some business deal he bought his damned title. Because no real society accepts him."

"Oh Dolo, the real society is gone. Finished. Except for a few seventy-year-old dowagers. You take a good look at today's society, gay Princes and Lords, rock stars, plus any beast from the States with over ten million! Even movie stars make it! And you, my dear, you're not social anymore, you're a celebrity. You're on all the magazine covers. God, the love story they're playing about you and Jimmy . . ."

"That's why I can't dash off into any social life."

"All right, then take a quiet lover. Only keep it that way. Love with your body . . . not your heart."

"Nita, do you really feel something for the Baron—besides his money and power?"

Nita turned away. "In the beginning, maybe it was just all the trimmings that attracted me. I mean if he had just walked into a room as Joe Doe I might not even have noticed him. But he has a presence, and I guess I was accustomed to every man gravitating toward me. He didn't. And when he was introduced . . . he seemed unimpressed. So it became a challenge—then love. Yes, love! Dolo, I swear right now—if he didn't have a dime I would still want to go to bed with him."

"But he's almost sixty. And you're thirty-five."

"Yes." Nita smiled. "This is the month that we're both thirty-five. You go thirty-six in three weeks."

Dolores had smiled. "I remember when I hit thirty . . . how dreadful I felt. How each year became a curse. I was rushing toward forty and there was no way to stop it. Now suddenly it seems ludicrously young. I'm the widow of the ages . . . and I'm *only* thirty-six."

Thirty-six!

9. The Will

SHE had celebrated her birthday with the twins and Mary Lou. Betsy Minton had not come to New York with them. She had a boyfriend in Washington and wanted every weekend off to commute. Imagine a dried-out spinster of forty-eight wanting to have an affair every weekend! So she had let Betsy stay in Washington.

She had bought the ten-room duplex in the River View House sight unseen. Bought it when she was still in London with Nita. Two hundred and fifty thousand dollars. And it had been a steal. A ten-room duplex, not counting maids' quarters—a divorcing couple had to unload it immediately. It was worth much more.

She had inherited two TV sets with the apartment, some drapes, and a few good pieces of furniture which she had re-covered. The next six months she spent with decorators

. . . that had really kept her occupied. She wanted it to be really beautiful. And it was. She turned and stared at the beautiful living room. It was a real salon. But for what? She still wasn't allowed to entertain. Next week would mark a year . . . and then she was attending a memorial with Michael as her escort. That was a big thrill. The rare times she did go out in public, dressed in navy or black, Michael was her escort. And she knew there were rumors that there was more than a brother-in-law/sister-in-law relationship. That was a real laugh. Michael, who always sat across the room when he came to visit her.

But where could she go? To lunch with her mother-in-law. Bridget was really cutting loose now. Timothy Ryan was bedridden with arthritis and had round-the-clock nurses. Bridget was healthy and had always loved the theater and concerts and she came to New York every week for two days. So Dolores would dutifully lunch with Bridget, go to the theater with her, with the constant Secret Service men in attendance. The only thing she enjoyed was the unbelievable publicity these rare outings caused. Jacqueline Onassis was already established "news" like Elizabeth Taylor. Now, *she*, Dolores Ryan, was the new glamour girl of the world. Funny . . . in the past, when she was a debutante, there were big movie stars who held the public's fancy—

Doris Day, Rita Hayworth, Lana Turner, Marilyn. Today, there were rock groups . . . and Dolores Ryan. She had made ten fan magazines in the course of this month.

She paced back into the den and stared at the river. And now she had financial problems to top it all. The lawyer had just left. The children's trust fund was in order, but, according to the will, Jimmy's money was to be added to their trust and she was to receive thirty thousand a year tax-free until his million-dollar trust came due. If Jimmy had still been alive, he'd be forty-three. That meant she wouldn't get the million for another seventeen years. But meanwhile how could she live on thirty thousand a year? After the will was read, Bridget insisted on paying for the apartment. "Look, my dear, personally I don't think you were properly cared for in the will. But then Jimmy was so young; and the least I can do is give you and the children a suitable place to live. Washington would hold dreadful memories for you now. I think New York is a wise move. I will also pay the maintenance for the apartment and for the children's schools. The thirty thousand should take care of your own needs very nicely."

It was a generous gesture, and she was grateful, but did Bridget know she had to pay one hundred and fifty dollars a week to her social secretary, who was still answering condolence letters from all over the world? There was also one hundred and fifty dollars a week for the children's nurse. Eighty-five dollars for a daily cleaning woman, one hundred and fifty dollars for a cook-housekeeper, plus Mr. Evans, who came twice a week for the heavy cleaning. That was an extra forty dollars a week. The food, no matter how she economized, ran over two hundred dollars a week. These expenses alone came to more than forty thousand a year. Christmas to the building employees was another small fortune. The limousines she hired were sixteen dollars an hour . . . the twins were in an expensive nursery school . . . Bridget just didn't realize. She couldn't do "very nicely" on thirty thousand a year.

And the rare times she went to lunch with the one girl she could almost call a friend . . . Janie Jensen . . . who had been Janie Birch at Finch . . . Janie had always been enormously rich but she and Janie had liked one another at school. Money hadn't seemed to matter then. Only now Janie was married to the Swedish Ambassador and Janie was very rich—because Svend Jensen was rich, too—and like the very rich, on the occasions they did have lunch, Janie insisted they take turns paying the check. And often she would go with Janie and watch her buy all the new styles and stare like a little girl while Halston or Valentino would say, "Oh, Mrs. Ryan, this is *so* right for you!" She could visualize herself in the creations as she watched the bulging Janie push her way into them, and she would say demurely, "No clothes now . . . I'm still . . ." Then she'd pause and they would nod understandingly.

10. Eddie

EVERYONE thought she had millions. The whole situation was ludicrous. She couldn't go to some inexpensive boutique for clothes. It would be in the papers immediately. Everyone would accuse her of being chintzy. She still took Mary Lou and the twins to the best children's place on Madison Avenue.

She attended the ceremonies of the anniversary of her husband's death in Washington. Then she came home . . . and stared at her wardrobe. All those outdated midi dresses. For the past year, she had lived in about six new "mourning outfits." But the closets full of clothes from "before" were out. The midi had been a huge flop! And she had two closets full. Even cutting them didn't work. The "look" was wrong.

She began taking long walks . . . wearing slacks. Photographers snapped her and somehow she came off looking sleek and dashing. She cycled in the park with Mary Lou after school when the weather permitted. She met Eddie Harris when Mary Lou fell off her bicycle in the park. The Secret Service man rushed to pick her up but Eddie, who was coming the other way, grabbed the child first. Dolores recognized him immediately. He was a brilliant young screenwriter (she often snuck into movies in the afternoon with a bandana and dark glasses).

He introduced himself. She smiled regally and he asked if he could cycle the rest of the way with them. By the end of the day they were good friends. She felt that he was a homosexual even though he was reputed to have had affairs with many women. She felt asexual toward him but she liked him and respected his talent.

"Listen," he said eagerly. "How about going to Leonard Bernstein's concert with me next week?"

"I'm afraid I can't," she said.

"Why? Afraid to make your first public appearance with a Jew?" He grinned.

"I never thought of your being anything other than a very talented man. It's just that my mother-in-law is coming in for the week and I'm spending some time with her in the country with friends. But the following week, would you come to my apartment for dinner? Just wear what you're wearing now . . . let's say a week from Tuesday."

He seemed thrilled at the offer and they
cycled across town to the River View House.
"Tenth floor," she said.

"What apartment?"

"I have the whole floor," she said. Her
innocent little girl expression covered the blatant remark. Then she quickly added, "What
is your favorite food? I have a marvelous cook
who is growing tired of preparing lamb chops
for the children."

"Spaghetti . . . marinara, minestrone.
And a salad."

"Fine. Eight o'clock. The children will
be in bed by then."

She thought about him for the rest of
the day. He had hit home with that remark—
"Afraid to make your first public appearance
with a Jew?" He was right . . . and he was
wrong. The Jewish part had nothing to do with
it. If an important Governor or Senator was
Jewish, she wouldn't hesitate to go out with
him . . . but to go out for the first time with
someone in show business . . . No! It wouldn't
fit her image.

She discussed it with Bridget, who
nodded solemnly while she ate her lunch.
"You were quite right. I'll speak to Michael.
He'll find you a suitable escort."

And she did attend an opening of a
museum the following week with a suitable
escort. The unmarried Chief Justice, who was
fifty-nine. It was the most boring night of her

life and she had spent five hundred on a Stavropoulos gown . . . wholesale. Her new social secretary, Nancy Kind, had arranged this.

She went to bed with Eddie Harris the
first night he came to her apartment. Possibly
because she felt it was clandestine, also she had
been positive he was a homosexual and someone she would never see again. She felt relaxed
and reached a climax for the first time in her
life. When they began she had pretended to
feel something, as she had done with Jimmy.
(Moan a bit . . . and get the thing over with.)
But Eddie had laughed. "You'd never make it
in the theater. Now relax and enjoy yourself."
Then he continued making love to her until
she fell back limp and exhausted.

She began to see him every week . . .
then twice a week . . . and then he suddenly
stopped calling her. She waited a week and
phoned him.

He was charming and when she asked
him to dinner he said, "Sure, but it's my turn."

"What do you mean?"

"To take you out to dinner."

"I . . . I can't, Eddie."

"Oh sure! But you can go to '21' with
Chief Justice Blinger and to Elaine's with a
poet who is old enough to be your grandfather."

"Those were two functions I was obliged
to attend. I was bored sick."

"What makes you think I'm not bored
coming to your apartment, drinking vintage

wine from Steuben glasses, eating a gourmet meal, and then servicing you in bed."

She slammed down the phone.

The next day he sent flowers and the following day she accepted his phone call. "Listen," he said eagerly, "there's a big party being given by the Mayor for some kind of Betterment of New York jazz. All your kind of right people will be there. Will you go with me?"

"I received an invitation," she said. "But—"

"But what? Listen, Dolores, it's either you go to the party with me or I take someone else . . . and we call it quits."

"I don't like parties," she said. "I never liked large parties, even at the White House." (Why was she explaining to this man! Because he was her only flesh and blood contact with the outside world.)

"Well, try this one for size. It's only Gracie Mansion . . . but we here in New York call it home."

"All right, Eddie."

11. Barry

SHE bought another Stavropoulos gown for the party. She had the hairdresser come to her house. She wore her one pair of diamond earrings. Jimmy had never been lavish with jewelry. He claimed it didn't fit their image. He never allowed her to wear fur . . . but the gown came with a coat, and it was early fall. Somehow, she would have to get a sable coat. The mink Bridget had bought her after Jimmy's death was out of style. It amused her how everyone put her on their best-dressed lists.

The party was in full swing, but when she arrived she felt the immediate hush and then the sudden murmur that ran through the room. The Mayor greeted her as if she were visiting royalty. He was obviously very friendly with Eddie Harris because he shook his hand vigorously and said, "I give you points for bringing the most beautiful lady in the world to Gracie Mansion."

For the next half hour it was a maze of introductions. Her back ached as she stood erect and accepted each new face with a firm handshake. And through it all she sensed someone across the room—someone who lounged against the wall lazily and seemed amused at the whole procedure. When everyone had been presented, he ambled over. Her first thought was, "He's incredibly handsome . . . is he in pictures . . . where have I seen him before?"

"Hi," he said, not bothering to hold out his hand. "I think it's about time we met. We have a lot in common."

"We have?" She was using the husky voice now. For some crazy reason she wanted to please this tall handsome man.

He pulled up a chair and she noticed he did it with a peculiar ease, an ease that Eddie Harris lacked—an ease that comes with years of breeding or being in the public eye.

"You came into power being married to a President," he smiled. "I lost my power being the son of a vice-president."

She smiled. Of course. It was Barry Haines. His father had been vice-president and had died of a heart seizure when he was running for President. And he would have made it. Bennington Haines, Sr., had great magnetism. His three daughters had been beautiful and made brilliant marriages. Barry Haines, Jr., was better-looking than anyone in the family. In fact, his looks had hurt his political career. When he ran for Mayor of New York, he lost to a dreary "party" man. People felt a man who looked like Barry Haines couldn't be a brilliant politician. Then he had run for the House of Representatives, lost that, and finally married a woman worth many millions. He was supposed to be connected with an important law firm, but his marriage to Constance McCoy had destroyed any chance he had of making people take him seriously. Constance McCoy had been married twice before. She was soigné, elegantly dressed, but not actively beautiful. Her appearance was one of bland understated chic. But she was the Hap Hap cereal heiress. She was across the room now talking to the Mayor. Everyone knew Constance only married Barry Haines for his name because she wanted children to carry on the Haines name. So far, she had suffered two miscarriages. She was in her forties, yet she was determined to keep trying.

All these thoughts flashed through Dolores' mind as her eyes met the gray eyes of Barry Haines. His stare was so direct that she felt the color come to her face.

She quickly presented Eddie Harris and both men acknowledged they had met before. There was a small orchestra playing in the other room. The music was soft and easy. Barry Haines' eyes had never wavered, even when he accepted the "introduction" to Eddie.

"Want to dance?" he said slowly.

"I . . ." She hadn't danced in years.

"Excuse us, Ed," he said as he took her arm and led her to the floor.

For a few minutes they danced in silence. Then he said, "Relax. You're trying to lead me. At least this is the one thing I do well. God knows I had to attend enough debutante balls. I should have medals for all the oxen I pushed around."

"Do you feel you're pushing me around?"

He laughed. "My lady, no one in the world could ever push *you* around. I doubt whether even your esteemed husband ever did that."

She chose not to answer but relaxed a bit and tried to follow his steps. Actually, she wasn't a good dancer—she had never had time to learn to dance. After her own debut, when most girls were attending parties every night, she had taken a job. And most of the men she met wanted to sit in quiet restaurants and talk.

"Hate me?" he asked.

"Why should I?"

"Well, you're not exactly pouring out any charm."

"Why should I? You're a married man."

"Oh, you mean charm is reserved just for unmarried men. I didn't realize you were husband-hunting."

"I don't want to walk off and leave you alone on the floor," she said quietly. "So please take me back to Eddie."

"With pleasure." He deftly led her through the crowd and when he brought her to Eddie Harris he said, "Thank you for the dance." He smiled at Dolores. "You didn't disappoint me—you're exactly as charming as I thought you'd be." Then he crossed the room.

She thought about the incident for several days. She refused all of Eddie Harris's calls. Somehow she could no longer take the idea of going to bed with him.

She wanted to go to bed with Barry Haines!

That was it!

12. America's Queen Victoria

SUBCONSCIOUSLY, she had known it all along. But he was a married man. She felt herself smiling. It never stopped Jimmy. She had been "Caesar's wife." Imagine reaching thirty-six and only having two men in your life. Your dead husband and Eddie Harris.

Perhaps she should give a cocktail party. A small one. Invite the Chief Justice, Leonard Bernstein, the Mayor, Eddie . . . and the Barry Haineses. No, that would be too obvious.

For the next few weeks she accepted dates with the Chief Justice, attended an opening of a show with Michael . . . (She had put in a hurried call to Washington, wanted his advice on schools for the children. They were in parochial schools, but she wondered if boarding school might not be the answer for Mary Lou; she was getting too tomboyish living with just the twins for company.)

She went to several art shows with the

Chief Justice—she went every place where she
thought she might run into Barry Haines. Each
outing brought her unbelievable publicity. But
no Barry Haines.

She had several boring lunches with
Janie Jensen, and subtly mentioned his name.
Janie wasn't any help. "He's one of life's mis-
fits, darling. His father was really a great man
. . . could have been President. And everyone expected such big things of Barry, and
Barry expected such big things of his father—
like leaving him a fortune. Well, the old man
did leave money, but by the time it was taxed
and divided between his sisters and himself,
he only had a quarter of a million. And the
idiot lived off the principal. Naturally, it was
gone in two years. He's with a law firm, but
since he barely squeezed through Harvard, he's
just there for the family name. Doesn't make
too much money—that's why he married Constance McCoy. I mean a Haines would never
marry a McCoy. Her father started as a pack-
ager in a cereal plant . . . invented one of his
own . . . got backing . . . became a millionaire with Hap Hap cereal . . . it's a good
cereal . . . I've tried it . . . I often eat it before going to bed . . . but it still doesn't make
her anything but the daughter of a shanty Irish
father."

"So was my husband—and my children."

"Ah, but darling, Jimmy was an excep-
tion. All the Ryans are. And children take their

mother's religion and heritage. Your children have fine Castilian blood. But Barry—" She sighed. "The Haines blood is so good—it's sad that he had to mix it with the McCoys'. So far they have no children . . . let's hope they don't. It's really a race of mongrels we're growing in the States. I mean even animals are purebred . . . when they mismate, they're put in pounds or put to sleep. You remember when my Princess Sha Sha accidentally got out in Darien and met that poodle. Oh God, the offspring. A mixture of pomeranian and poodle . . . I had the little horrors put to sleep immediately."

"But aren't mongrel dogs supposed to be the brightest?"

"That's a fallacy. You don't see any dray horses running in races. All they can do is pull hansoms through the park. A Secretariat comes from years of good blood . . . that's how champions are made. God knows I was once attracted to a movie star . . . I could have married him . . . he had money too. But I chose Svend. Svend is descended from royalty. Which reminds me, I know that Eddie Harris is terribly talented and attractive . . . but I heard his mother speaks with an accent."

"I take people as I find them—not what their mothers or fathers are like. And I imagine my great-grandmother spoke English with a heavy accent."

"Ah, but darling . . . that was a Spanish accent . . . and there's a big difference."

"I haven't seen Eddie lately."

"Dolores, it's time you thought about your future and the children and forgot about people like Eddie."

"I don't understand."

"Well, I can see the man's attraction . . . his talent . . . his bohemian friends . . . but you must realize you can never remarry."

"I hadn't thought about it. But why couldn't I? I mean if the right person came along?"

"Oh . . . if a Prince or a King . . . or an unmarried President . . . the public might accept that. But darling, you are America's Queen Victoria. The public worshiped you and Jimmy together . . . they suffer your bereavement . . . they love your children. Oh darling, I used to watch you both and secretly get jealous—he was so handsome . . . and you were so beautiful."

Were?!? Dolores managed to show no emotion. But that night she studied her face in the mirror. She was approaching thirty-seven. Thirty-seven—too old to be a highly eligible single girl, but much too young to stay alone for the rest of her life. And live up to an image that didn't really exist. God, the public must have known about Jimmy and that movie star, the girl who still talked about it to everyone— it even got her bigger billing in pictures. And Tanya—Tanya was now having an affair with a famous orchestra conductor. But Tanya didn't have an image to live up to. Queen Victoria! Victoria was a fat little woman and Albert had been her prince consort . . . and he had been true to her. But *she* had always walked in the wake of Jimmy's footsteps . . . closed her eyes when he had other women.

13. Horatio

AND now she wanted Barry Haines. The more she thought about it, the more obsessive the feeling became. Yet how could she reach him? She had no privacy. Photographers were parked outside her building. Could she spend the rest of her life going to dreary openings with a Chief Justice or Sir Warren Stanford, who had been introduced to her by Michael? Sir Warren was a widower, but he didn't have any real money. A beautiful home outside of London . . . and four small children of his own. He had hinted marriage but she couldn't see herself stuck in the English countryside raising *his* children and her own.

Sometimes she paced the apartment at night. She took to listening to disc jockeys and watching the Late Late movies. She read every novel on the best-seller list. She cycled in the park when the weather was good. She took the children to Bridget's farm in Virginia

for Thanksgiving and holidays where Michael
would come with his wife and their kids, and
the sisters with their children and husbands.
But she was always alone. Sometimes she wondered about Bridget . . . the way she went to
Mass every day . . . the way she took long
walks . . . she was in her seventies but her
husband had been sick for fifteen years. Did
the urge for sex stop in the fifties? Or did
Bridget's faith in religion carry her through?
Timothy Ryan was practically a vegetable now.
He was so gnarled from arthritis and his face
was so puffed from the cortisone that he pre-
ferred to remain in his room most of the time.

She decided to give her first party that
spring. She spent weeks going over the list.
Janie Jensen helped her. She slipped in the
Haineses in a casual way and was relieved
when Janie agreed.

The invitations were engraved by Tiffany's. Thirty-five people had been invited
. . . cocktails and a buffet supper . . . June
first. She let her social secretary address them
but when it came to Mr. and Mrs. Barry
Haines, she crossed out her printed name, and
said, "Am looking forward to seeing you both—
Dolores."

The acceptances poured in immediately.
Society columnists got wind of it and began
writing about the coming party. The night of
the party Constance Haines called to tell her

that she would be delighted to come, but would it be all right if she had her cousin escort her . . . Barry had the flu and was running 102 temperature.

Dolores was almost suicidal, but her charm never wavered. The building outside was cluttered with the press and photographers. It was truly the social event of the season. Yet her only happy moment came when Constance said, "As soon as Barry gets well, you must come to our place for dinner."

The following day, the papers were filled with the famous society figures who were photographed as they came into her building. The party made news for three days. Dolores wrote and rewrote ten "Get well" notes to Barry . . . then tore them up.

She was in the midst of supervising the sewing of name tapes in Mary Lou's summer camp clothes when the cable came from Nita. FIND ME A TEN OR TWELVE ROOM APARTMENT IN NEW YORK. AM ARRIVING IN TWO WEEKS TO LIVE THERE. WILL EXPLAIN ALL WHEN I SEE YOU. IF HORATIO CAPON CALLS YOU TELL HIM I'LL BE IN ON SUNDAY. HE CAN MEET ME AT THE AIRPORT. I KNOW IT WOULD CAUSE TOO MUCH COMMOTION IF YOU DID. I'LL NEED A GOOD BUTLER, A PERSONAL SECRETARY, AND A FEW MAIDS. LOVE, NITA.

Before she had time to think, the phone rang and a lisping voice announced itself as

Horatio Capon. She knew his work. He had
painted some excellent seascapes and the art
critics had given him raves. But he hadn't had
an exhibition in years. He had become a television personality—looked like a blondish pig,
but gushingly told outrageous stories and gossip. "Oh, Dolores Ryan," he cooed. "What a
pleasure . . . I mean . . . I've known Nita a
long while . . . we met in England when I
had a showing there . . . and I've always
wanted to meet you. Have you seen my work?"

"Not recently," Dolores said.

"Well, to tell the truth, I've had a block.
I've been working on a *huuuge* canvas . . .
and I keep painting out and redoing certain
figures. And then I must admit, I've become a
sort of social butterfly. I mean an extra man is
always *so* in demand . . . especially when he's
a celebrity."

"Well . . . I just received Nita's cable
and—"

"Oh, let's go apartment hunting together. It will be such giggles."

"I have to think about it," she said. "I
want to call my real estate agent first."

"But darling, we could have a few
lunches together. You must be lonely."

"Not really," Dolores said. "Just busy.
Getting three children ready for camp, along
with settling things for Nita, will take even
more of my time."

"But love . . . I'm a whiz at apartments. I know all the right buildings and we could have a ball."

"Well, if my real estate agent doesn't come up with something—where can I reach you?"

"Who knows?" he simpered. "I have an apartment on Fifth . . . just a *pied-à-terre* . . . five rooms. A house in Quogue, and one of the most heavenly flats in London. You see, I can take them all off my income tax as this is my official residence. So I just flit about. I'm afraid I'll have to call you."

"When do you paint?" Dolores asked.

"That's a good question." He giggled. "But one day I'll just put an end to all these parties and television shows. You know they've offered me my own show . . . but one day I will close the door on the world and finish the masterpiece of all time."

"Well, I wouldn't want to keep you from your work . . ."

"It's a pleasure," he gushed. "With our little Nitzi arriving, I couldn't work anyhow. The little darling is with me constantly when I'm in London. You know," and now his voice grew confidential, "she *has* to come here. Lord Nelson has dumped the Swiss journalist for a young Italian Princess who is only twenty-two . . . Princess Elena Elmanico . . . she's absolutely divine . . . and Lord Nelson takes her everywhere openly . . . she makes poor Nitzi look dowdy. I told her to come here . . .

between you and me, we must give her some new glamour."

Dolores hung up the phone slowly. Poor Nita . . .

14. A Possession

IT was a muggy day in July when Nita arrived. There had been many phone calls from Horatio, but Dolores hadn't accepted them. She found a marvelous apartment for Nita on Fifth Avenue . . . fifteen rooms . . . and since it was obvious that Nita had plenty of money, she hired an excellent staff. She ordered mattresses and springs . . . she figured that decorating the apartment would do Nita good . . . and she would do it with her. She looked forward to Nita being here . . . she'd have someone to talk to whom she could trust . . . someone to lunch with every day . . . someone to talk out her loneliness to.

She hired a limousine and with a Secret Service man met Nita's plane. TWA allowed her to drive onto the runway . . . and Nita was whisked through Customs. She took Nita to her new apartment and Nita nodded absently.

"Of course, it's bare," Dolores said en-

thusiastically. "But Nita, think of the fun we
can have furnishing it."

Nita nodded dully. "I've got to get it
done by fall when I send for the children.
Nelson has them in a French camp." She
opened her purse and took out a flat pillbox
and swallowed a little white pill. "Pheno,"
Nita said with an attempt at a smile. "The
doctor thinks it will help me."

"Nelson will get over this girl," Dolores
said. When Nita didn't answer, Dolores hurried on. "Look, Jimmy had a lot of romances.
Only Tanya was important. Once a man gets
over the big one . . . if you ignore the rest,
they soon die a natural death. Besides, no beautiful young girl is going to stick with Nelson
when she knows there's no chance of divorce.
It was the same with Jimmy—only the secrecy
and intrigue involved sometimes made the
affair last longer."

Nita continued to gaze absently. Dolores
suddenly put her arms around her. "Oh, Nita,
it's not the end of the world."

"It is," Nita said quietly. "And I don't
give a damn about Nelson and this girl. It's
Erick."

"The Baron? Is that still on?"

Nita held out her hand and Dolores
stared at a huge diamond.

"Thirty carats . . . his parting gift to
me."

"He's left you?"

Nita nodded. "A week ago. He told me he really loved Ludmilla Rosenko, and that she refused to stand for his liaison with me any longer. She wouldn't stand for *me!* Imagine losing out to a fifty-five-year-old woman."

"But she's very beautiful."

"Her face has been pulled so tight from so many lifts she can barely smile. But you see, Erick remembers her when she was a star, and he worships talent. That's the only thing that turns him on. Ludmilla was a star. He used to watch her night after night and dream about having her. It seems every man in Paris felt that way. And when he got her . . . he gave her everything. He's made her independently rich, so he knows she loves him . . ."

"But you're independently rich," Dolores said.

"But I have no name and no talent. Erick adores possessions. He's just bought a ship from the Germans—an ocean liner—and he's having it turned into a private yacht. It will be twice the size of anything Onassis or anyone else has. You see that will be a possession. Ludmilla is still revered . . . and she's a possession. So when she gave him the ultimatum . . . me or her . . . that was it."

"Oh Nita, I'm sorry. Perhaps it's for the best."

"Maybe . . . but I had to get away." She opened her purse and popped another pheno into her mouth.

"Nita . . . you shouldn't take them that often."

Nita smiled vaguely. "It's better than sitting around sobbing."

Dolores stood up. "Nita, you're staying with me until this place is done. And we'll have such fun. I'll give a party for you . . . invite fun people . . . and you'll have a big social life here. Then when your apartment is done, you can give parties. And we'll have a great time doing it. Just think—not having to stint on money . . . you've got more than you could use."

"Did Horatio call you?" Nita asked dully.

"Yes."

"Why didn't he come with you to meet the plane?"

"Nita, I'm the wife of a President. I can't associate with just anyone."

"Horatio isn't just anyone," Nita said slowly. "I admit he's a funny-looking little man. But I met him at several parties in London. He knows all the right people."

"I don't like him," Dolores said.

"How can you say that if you haven't met?"

"I've seen him simpering away on television . . . trying to be a wit . . . talking about every subject except the one he's supposed to know. Art. He's bitchy. I don't like him."

"He makes me laugh," Nita said. "And he's better to lunch with than any girl. He knows *all* the dirt."

Dolores stared at her sister. It was the first bit of enthusiasm Nita had shown. "All right, Nita. I'll have your Horatio to dinner one night."

The next month passed quickly. Dolores was a whirlwind of activity. She showed Nita swatches, she took measurements—and through it all she tried not to notice Nita's air of lethargy, as if she were on another planet, as if she didn't quite hear everything Dolores said. She even went to Orsini's for lunch with Nita and Horatio. Nita was right. He was a funny gossip and she enjoyed him. When Horatio was around, it seemed the one time Nita was "with it" and not in her usual dream-like state.

In September, the apartment was not finished but it was quite livable. Nita sent for the children and their nurse. The rest of the staff had been engaged by Dolores and they were excellent. Nita also hired a social secretary, a nice conscientious girl who developed a permanent worried look as Nita just let her sit in front of a typewriter for days, waiting for instructions. She met Horatio for lunch almost every day, and the third week in September, Dolores had a sit-down dinner for thirty in her honor.

The Barry Haineses accepted. It was a

good assortment of people. There was Eddie
Harris, who fascinated Nita, an opera star, two
Senators, a top designer, an English director,
an English actor from the cast of a hit show,
and the current top social names. She also invited Horatio Capon, who, to her amazement,
seemed to enthrall several women, including
a beautiful Wall Street broker's wife. Rita
Hellman was known as Super Elegance. She
had made the best-dressed list Hall of Fame,
and it seemed incongruous to watch her sitting
at Horatio's feet laughing at his gossip.

That night Nita called her when the
party was over. "Dolo . . . you've been so
good to me . . . we've never really been close
. . . but you've saved my life. I love you,
Dolo . . ." Her voice sounded vague.

"Nita, are you all right?"

"Yes . . . I just took a pheno. Dolo . . .
are you happy?"

"I am tonight—for the first time in almost two years."

"It was a wildly successful party."

"Nita . . . did you get to talk with
Barry Haines?"

"Yes, he's very good-looking."

"Nita—" Dolores paused. Then she said
quietly, "I'm mad about him."

This time Nita's voice was clear. "You
are . . . oh Dolo . . . great! How long has
this been going on?"

"Nothing has gone on . . . until tonight. He spent as much time with me as he could and told me he's been thinking of me all along too. He's coming here for tea. To-morrow!"

"Oh Dolo, I'm so happy for you."

15. A Proper Tea

FOR the next three weeks Dolores lived in a high state of excitement. She and Barry Haines had had a proper tea. Then he came by one night at nine (after the children were in bed) for a quiet dinner . . . and they had gone to bed together. It had been beyond anything Dolores dreamed it would be. She clung to him and told him she loved him. She said it over and over. Later when they sat before the fire in her bedroom, he said, "Dolores, you know if I got a divorce from Constance, I'd have no money. She has it all."

"But I could never marry a divorced man. It's against my religion. Besides, I don't have enough for both of us . . . even if you managed to get your marriage annulled."

"I thought you were a millionaire," he said.

She stared into the fire. "I get money each year from a trust but it's not enough. Of

course, the children will have several million
when they're grown . . . but I am not a millionaire."

"And I only make twenty thousand a
year at the firm."

"That's all!"

"Dolores, they're just paying me for the
use of my name on the door. I'm a lousy lawyer.
You see . . . my family . . . we were born
into politics. My grandfather was Mayor of this
city . . . my great-grandfather was in the Senate . . . my mother had money . . . but it
was all used for my father's campaign. Then
he died . . . and . . ."

"You married Constance."

He nodded. "Who will you marry?"

She shook her head. "No one. I am
Queen Victoria. Didn't you know that? I've
met a few Counts and Lords—all eligible, all
poor. They think *I* have money. Funny, isn't
it—how money is the great leveler."

"Can we go on together?" he asked.

"Forever." She threw her arms around
him. "Barry, when I said I loved you . . . that
wasn't in a fit of passion. I never even said that
to Jimmy. I love you and as long as I know I
can see you a few times a week . . . privately
. . . like this . . . then I can go on living out
the legend . . . using the Judge or Michael as
an escort to some dreary functions."

"Then why bother going to them at all?"

"Because I can't sit home every night."

She began to pace. "Barry, for almost two years I've lived like a caged animal. A year in mourning, going nowhere, eating with the children. This past year . . . going to boring functions . . . having lunch with my mother-in-law . . . whom I really like . . . Bridget is quite a lady. Then, coming back here . . . listening to the children's lessons . . . helping them . . . watching TV. I love beautiful clothes. I'm only thirty-seven. I want to wear them and be seen occasionally . . . so I go somewhere with Michael or the Judge."

"Don't ever break your image," he said as he ran his hand through her hair. (She had taken off the hairpiece, but fortunately he never noticed the difference.)

"What *is* my image really?" she asked.

"Like a cross between Garbo and royalty, totally inaccessible . . ."

She fell into his arms and kissed him. "How inaccessible do I seem now?" And they made love on the bear rug in front of the fireplace.

16. The Pills

SHE called Nita the following day and insisted on lunching with her. "Without Horatio!" she said.

They sat in a quiet restaurant, and Dolores told her about Barry. Nita listened vaguely and then said, "Dolo, you sound like a schoolgirl."

"But Nita, he's the only man I've ever really loved."

"What about Jimmy?"

Dolores seemed thoughtful. "I was terribly attracted to him when we met. But you know how Mother kept downing the Irish . . . it sort of took away his glamour. After all, he wasn't President then. No one dreamed he would be . . . and it was time I was getting married . . . you had taken Nelson and—"

"Taken Nelson!"

Dolores lit a cigarette to hide the color that came to her face. "I can tell you now,

Nita, but at nineteen I was mad for him."

"Oh God . . ." Nita shivered. "He's nothing in bed. I knew it before I married him but then, as you say, we did listen to Mother, and we weren't exactly rich."

"You went to bed with him before you married him?"

"Dolo, I went to bed with a boy in the back of a car when I was fifteen. Now don't try to tell me you were a virgin when you married Jimmy."

Dolores smiled. "I haven't had too many extracurricular affairs." (She couldn't bring herself to admit to Nita that Barry was only the third man in her life.)

"Are you going to marry him?" Nita asked.

Dolores shook her head. "Constance has all the money."

Nita shrugged. "Well, at least you've got yourself a good lover, which is more than I can say. I tried that screenwriter you admire . . . a big zero . . . he wants to talk all the time. Makes love just to get it over with, then actually reads you scenes from his new play." Nita yawned. "Come back to the apartment. My new bedroom rug has arrived . . . and there are a few other things you haven't seen."

Nita signed the check and then popped one of her phenos into her mouth. Dolores decided Nita's vagueness was caused by the phenos. Yet she had asked her own doctor about them and he said one or two a day couldn't really hurt her.

Dolores reveled in the luxury of Nita's new apartment. "Oh Nita. . . those mirrors . . . where did you get them?"

"I had them shipped from England. Dolo, you should really marry money. You're like a cat. You revel in it. I'd be just as happy in a hotel suite as I am in this apartment. I don't even care about clothes."

The phone rang. Nita saw the second light. "I'll take it. That's Horatio . . . on my private line. Dolo, go into my bedroom. I just got two Valentino suits and they're a bit too large. Try them. If they fit, take them." She picked up the phone.

Like a child Dolores ran into the bedroom. She sat on the edge of the bed for a moment. It reminded her of her days at the White House, when she redecorated without thought of cost, thinking Jimmy wouldn't care what she would spend. Then she went to the closet. The Valentinos were hanging apart. She stared enviously at all the clothes and furs Nita had. She took out the suits and tried them on. They fit perfectly. She changed back into her own suit. The light on the phone was still on . . . her own apartment was beautiful . . . but nothing like this. Suddenly her head began to ache. Why did money rule the world? If she had money she could pull strings and maybe get Barry an annulment. Yet Nita wasn't happy with all her money.

She went into the bathroom to get an aspirin. When she opened the medicine chest, she stared in amazement. There was bottle after bottle of every kind and color of sleeping pills. Red ones . . . yellow ones . . . the two-toned ones (the kind Jimmy used to take if he had a big press session on TV . . . when he said he wanted and needed a good night's sleep). Then she saw all the bottles of white pills . . . the pheno Nita used. She reached for one . . . maybe it would make her feel better. She stared at the label. But it wasn't pheno. It said, "For Pain . . . Demerol." She knew about Demerol. They had given it to her when she lost the second set of twins and she had floated in a misty twilight, feeling no pain . . . nothing.

Good God, was Nita on Demerol? Was that why she was always so vague? She walked into the living room. Nita was curled on the couch giggling at some news Horatio was telling her. She reached into Nita's pocketbook and opened her pillbox. Like a panther, Nita was on top of her. "What are you doing?"

"I have a headache. I want one of your phenos."

Nita grabbed the box. "They're not for headaches." She rang a bell and from nowhere

102

a maid appeared. "Get Mrs. Ryan some aspirin." Then she went back to the phone call with Horatio, clutching the pillbox in her hand.

17. Gossip

DOLORES worried about Nita for two days. But on the third day she had a bigger worry. Barry burst in late that afternoon with a newspaper in his hand. "Have you seen this?"

Dolores shook her head. "I never read columns," she said. (She read them avidly, but she hadn't seen the papers that day.)

"Listen to this. 'What untouchable glamorous lady is very in touch with the handsome husband of a very rich lady? Since they both come from political backgrounds, maybe it's just politics they talk about in those late-night get-togethers.'"

"I . . . it could be anyone," Dolores said.

"But it's us."

"I know, but Constance will never believe it," she pleaded.

"That isn't it. What worries me is how did it get in the columns? We haven't been anywhere publicly . . . your maids are always asleep. Where is the leak?"

She didn't want to put the thought into words, or even allow it to form in her mind. But she knew it was Nita. Nita was the only one who knew. But Nita wouldn't tell a gossip columnist. Yet would Nita tell Horatio? Oh God . . . *no!* But she would have to test her.

"Let me track it down," she said evenly. "I think I know where the leak is—and I'll plug it immediately. Go home. I'll see you tomorrow night."

She had lunch with Nita the following day. "I've split with Barry," she said casually.

"Three days ago you were out of your mind about him," Nita said.

"Last night, Eddie Harris came over. We went to bed together. Oh Nita . . . he was divine."

"He *is* very earthy. Only he talks about his work too much. But he is single—and available. Think about it, Dolo."

"Oh, I couldn't marry Eddie Harris!"

"Why not? If things get dull he can always read you his new movie script like he did with me."

Dolores grew misty-eyed. "When we made love he recited poetry to me. Poetry he made up, just for me. Oh Nita, it's such a shame I can't marry him. He's been divorced—the Church would never stand for it."

Two days later in the same gossip col-

umn there was another "blind item." "Our untouchable glamorous lady is really *not* that
untouchable. Now she's dropped the other
lady's husband for a very eligible screenwriter."

Dolores stared at it. Nita! But why?

She picked up the phone immediately.
"Nita, why did you do it?"

Nita sounded vague. "Oh, you mean the
two Valentinos I sent over to you. Well, they
were too big for me and—"

"I got them and thanks. I have no pride
. . . I accept being the poor relative. No, I'm
talking about the column . . . there's a blind
item in the paper about Eddie and me."

"Well . . . that can't hurt you."

"Nita, did you give it out?"

"*No!*"

"I don't believe you."

"Dolo . . . I swear . . . I . . . I told
Horatio . . . and I know he's a professional
gossip, but it never dawned on me that he
would say anything."

"And you also told him about me and
Barry . . ."

"I . . . I might have. You know, I take
a drink with the phenos at lunch . . . and
then I float. I can't remember what I say."

"Nita, they aren't phenos. They're Demerol. Why are you on them?"

"I—I sprained my back when I was ski-
ing, and I take them occasionally."

"Nita, what are you doing to yourself?"

"Trying to get through each day, the

same as you are. Only I don't have one exciting lover after another." And Nita slammed down the phone.

Dolores wasn't as upset about the column mention as she was about Nita. She had looked forward to Nita's arrival. And for the first time they had met as equals and she had felt a closeness; now she realized the closeness had only been in her mind. Nita was caught up in some kind of drug-sedated lethargy and couldn't be trusted with any confidences. So once again she was alone. Except for Barry Haines.

If her relationship with Nita became more superficial (Dolores refused to go to lunch if Horatio was along), her attachment to Barry Haines became more intense. She forced herself to go to "important small dinner parties" with Eddie Harris, the Judge, or Michael as an escort. And she was aware that there was great speculation about her relationship with Michael. She did nothing to dispel it for by now she realized that talk, any kind of talk, only added to the legend she had become. But when she was alone with Barry, those three wonderful nights a week, the world closed in, and there were just the two of them.

18. Love

A YEAR passed and she began to wonder when she would get control of the "Barry" situation. Usually with crushes, she grew weary of them and took the commanding position—like with Eddie Harris. He had not been allowed to touch her since Barry, but he was so eager to be with her he took her on any terms. And even Michael was quick to spring at any engagement when she needed an important escort. His wife, Joyce, took it all in good grace. (Personally, Joyce found Dolores very stilted and dull and she understood that Michael felt playing escort to her on an important occasion was his duty.)

During the year, Nita flew back to London twice, once to keep things looking "right" with Nelson—going to all the proper balls—and the second time to make one last plea to the Baron. She had returned more depressed than ever.

"Erick wants no part of me," she had said, sobbing, to Dolores. "I practically got on my knees and begged him. How can he want that old ballerina?"

"Nita," Dolores said, trying to comfort her, "does it occur to you that Erick is sixty-one? And Ludmilla is over fifty! You're young. You want sex. Maybe Erick is slowing down— maybe he can't do it as often as you would like and maybe Ludmilla is content to accept him on any terms."

"I'd accept him with sex only once a week . . . on any terms, too."

But Nita found a new set of friends and a few new lovers. She still lunched with Horatio, and still occasionally went to Dolores' in tears over Erick . . . but she bought clothes, attended parties, and soon became a regular of the Beautiful People scene.

Life settled down to a comfortable routine for Dolores. Her public life was sparse enough to make any outing a major event. Even if she went to an offbeat place like the Ginger Man with Bridget, she would find all the reporters and photographers waiting outside. They would follow her on her bike rides with the twins and Mary Lou. Mary Lou was becoming a problem. She was nine now and wanted to dress in leotards and plaid skirts. Dolores was trying to keep her young-looking —and Mary Lou was growing so fast and putting on weight. She solved the clothes problem by switching her to an excellent Catholic school where they all wore uniforms. But only the moments spent with Barry Haines counted. They saw each other every day . . . even if he just dropped by for a martini . . . or a quick lunch . . . and then there were always the three nights they had together. Constance believed in the "weekly law meeting," the one night he played squash, and his poker night. Actually, Constance didn't really care. She played backgammon, had a multitude of friends, was on many charities, and spent all her winters in Palm Beach.

Winter was their best time . . . and their worst. They were together every night, except for the weekends when he had to fly to Palm Beach and on the holidays. Christmas and New Year's without Barry was agonizing. But there were good times in the winter when he taught the children how to make popcorn around the fire. And when they all trimmed the tree (true, it *was* a week before Christmas), and in a way, it made up for the loneliness of Christmas and New Year's Eve without him.

He genuinely adored the twins and Mary Lou. Mary Lou had a giant-sized crush on him and would go out of her way to have a problem with math and bring it to him. Oddly enough, it annoyed Dolores to see Mary Lou snuggle on Barry's lap in her bathrobe.

She was overdeveloped for her age, and was beginning to grow breasts. Dolores had very small breasts but she could see Mary Lou was going to be amply endowed. And when she grew older and lost the "baby fat," she'd be magnificent.

Their evenings together were usually harmonious and filled with love. At ten o'clock, she'd make a big show in front of the servants of seeing him out. Then in fifteen minutes she'd pretend to go to the door to see if the papers had been dropped, and Barry would sneak back in. He would remain overnight, rising at six in time to slip out before the servants or children got up; go to his apartment; shave and change and go to the office. And once he was there, he would call her and wake her up at ten by telling her he loved her.

She refused to join any committees or charities. She did participate in Bridget's charity for homeless pregnant girls, but that only took one afternoon a month. She knew the press speculated on her loneliness . . . on her rare luncheons with Bridget, Janie Jensen, or Nita.

Nita also sent her clothes. She would go out of her way to buy something a "bit too large" but Dolores knew it was because she felt sorry for her. She had told Nita that her affair with Eddie Harris was washed up, that they were just friends.

But as time passed and her obsession

with Barry grew, she began to have daydreams about their possible marriage. If she was careful, with his twenty thousand and her thirty, they *could* manage. *Perhaps* he *could* get an annulment.

19. Sisters

IN the spring, Nita decided to take another
quick trip to London to attend a round of
social events with Nelson. He had broken with
the Princess . . . there was someone else . . .
but it wasn't dreadfully important. Also Nelson
wanted to see the children. And she had just
posed for a top fashion photographer and would
be on the cover in New York and Paris of a
magazine called *Fashion.*

"It's breaking just in time," Nita said.
"Think of the publicity it will give me."

"Is that important to you?"

"It never was . . . before. Once I was
considered glamorous, a great beauty. Now I'm
just *your* sister. Everywhere I go people ask
me what you're *really* like. Everyplace I'm invited to in this country, I find I'm really invited
because I'm *your* sister. They even have the
temerity to ask me if I can manage to make
you come. There's one slob of a woman de-

signer who has offered me a whole wardrobe free, if I'll just bring you to one of her dinners. I'm going there tonight, and I know she'll make the offer again. She never gives up."

"Then why do you go?"

Nita shrugged. "Because she's a celebrity collector . . . and as much as I loathe her, she does have interesting guests. It's funny —they all hate her, but they come because they know everyone will be a 'name.' And I've met more quick darling 'romances' there."

"Nita, I never knew you were this promiscuous."

"I never was really. Oh, I lost my virginity ahead of you, but I think that was only because I was curious. But now I need these romances . . . these Sunday afternoons. Even though it was common knowledge in London that Nelson had a girl, I had a certain glamour. Here, I'm nothing—*you're* the big star now."

"But Nita, that's just because I was married to Jimmy."

"That may have started it. But it's more than that now. Jimmy's been dead almost four years. And your popularity has never been greater. You're on the cover of every magazine. You're like a goddess. The lonely lovely goddess . . . just spending her time with her children . . . taking long walks . . . the regal beauty . . . mysterious . . . aloof . . . glamorous. And me, with all the fantastic clothes and jewelry—I'm just *your* sister. It's even that

way in Europe now. Why do you think Nelson
wants me to come back! He even asked if you
could come."

"Maybe I could." (Easter was coming
. . . Barry would have to go to Palm Beach
. . . the lonely holidays again. . . .)

"No, I don't want you to come. I want
to be someone on my own. Why do you think I
permit Horatio the Horror around?"

"I thought he amused you."

"No, he's as phony as the others. But he
takes me to Pearl's, Elaine's and a lot of fun
places." Nita lit a cigarette. "But do you know
something—it's not fun anymore. Suddenly all
the faces seem the same, and suddenly I'm no
longer a big attraction. And Horatio—he's beginning to get on my nerves. That insane giggle
of his . . . his hands are always moist and he's
suddenly begun to drink a lot. But at least he
still treats me as if I'm really important. Incidentally, he hates you. He says you're a snob."

"Well, thank God I don't have to please
Horatio Capon."

"Oh, he's not important." Tears came to
Nita's eyes. "My life is such a mess, Dolo. I've
got nothing." Suddenly she fell into her sister's
arms and began to sob convulsively.

Dolores held her like a child and stroked
her hair. "You've got everything, Nita. That is,
you've got plenty to be thankful for. You've
got your husband. Granted it's not an ideal
marriage, but if anything went wrong, if you

or the children were sick, he'd be there. And
you've got wonderful children. A brilliant social life . . . plenty of money . . . and what's
more you can come and go as you please. And
Nita—people do know who you are."

"Yes, I'm Dolores Ryan's sister!"

"No. You are Lady Bramley, and a very
beautiful lady at that. And you've always been
far more beautiful than I. You've just been
locked away with Horatio too long."

Nita made a faint attempt at a smile.
Then Dolores said, "Nita, I've never asked a
favor of you in my life. But please . . . please
let me go back to London with you. I won't
go to any of the big parties—I don't have the
clothes for them—but I'd love to bring the
children there over the Easter holidays. It's a
lonely time for them without a father. We'd
stay at your place in the country."

"Oh, I can just see it," Nita said, sitting
up and daintily wiping the mascara from under
her eyes. "All the press at the airport. I'd
have to give a gala for you . . . and then that
would start the whole thing. Besides, I don't
want any responsibilities. I'm going to try to
see Erick. Maybe since all this time has passed,
maybe he missed me."

"But he must be sixty-two and—"

"And he's still virile. He's one of those
men who will still be enjoying sex at eighty.
Dolo, don't you see—my return will at least
give me an opening wedge with him. It falls

right on his birthday. I'll send him a gift. And if he's not in London, I'll fly to Paris or Rome or wherever he is. I hear his new ship is finished. It's supposed to be a miniature S.S. *France.*"

"I read about it in *Time.* They say he knocked out whole decks. There are seven master duplex suites, ten master bedrooms, three salons, a ballroom, an indoor and outdoor pool, a skating rink—he's the only man who turned an ocean liner into a private yacht."

"That's true. Oh Dolo, don't you see— I can't bring you to London. I'd be expected to be seen with you . . . have luncheon with you . . . tea . . . and a new rash of attention would be focused on me. The paparazzi would be after me, but not for *me*—for you. And the picture of me will break on the cover of *Fashion* just at that time. But with you there —on the cover of every magazine—it would rob me of my big moment."

Dolores sat beside her sister and held her hand. "Look, Nita, if you really love Erick, maybe it would be better if you played it loose."

Nita laughed. "You're a great one to be giving out advice on love."

"No, I realize that. But even I know that if you smother a man, he tries to break away. That's why European women are supposed to be such great mistresses . . . they know just how to hold the rein."

"It's easy for you to talk from theory,"

Nita said, as the tears came to her eyes again. "You don't know what it's like to lie awake nights and dream of a man. I know Erick is ugly by your standards. But Dolo, when he walks into a room, I get weak. He . . . he turns me on, as they say. Look, all this time has passed and I still think only of him."

"When are you leaving for London?" Dolores asked.

"Next week. Tell me—what can I get for a billionaire who has everything?"

"Erick?" Dolores seemed thoughtful. "I don't know."

"No, you wouldn't. You're really cold, aren't you, Dolores? We've never really been close or really known one another."

"What makes you think I'm cold?"

"Well, look at the record since Jimmy died. And let's face it, you never really held him . . . but now what have you done? You had a chance with one of the most attractive men in the world . . . Eddie Harris . . . and now he's dating some big glamour girl in Hollywood and it doesn't bother you. Then there's your affair with Barry Haines . . . What *do* you do with yourself?"

"I lunch with Bridget once a week. Timothy is failing; it would be so much better for Bridget if he died. I'll have to take the children to their farm for Easter, and it's so depressing to see him being lifted in and out of a wheelchair, or hear him moaning in pain.

Bridget is very strict—she'll only let him have his pain killer every four hours. . . ." Dolores paused. "Incidentally, Nita—you aren't still on Demerol?"

"Only when I'm bitterly unhappy and want to float. But I haven't had any for three days. I'm planning my campaign for Erick. I must have a clear head."

"Nita, I hope you get him back if that's what you really want."

"You really don't understand it, do you?"

"No. Because he's so unattractive and I have the feeling that title or not, he has no sensitivity . . . no deep emotion . . . and these are the things that make a woman really love a man."

Nita rose. "How would you know about love? Anyway, happy time in Virginia . . . and please, Dolo . . . wish me luck!"

20. The Bait

WHEN Nita left for London, Dolores fell into a deep depression. True, Nita had been with the Jet Set most of the winter, but she invariably came dashing back to Dolores every few weeks and they had lunched together and talked and she really felt they had a rapport. But now it had all come out. Nita didn't really like her. Tears came to her eyes. She had no one—no one who really cared. But that wasn't true . . . her children loved her . . . and Barry loved her . . . he was coming tonight for the last time for three weeks. He had to go to Palm Beach for the holidays with Constance.

She had been on the farm in Virginia for two days when the cable arrived from Nita. COME TO LONDON. WANT YOU AS HOUSE GUEST. WITH OR WITHOUT THE CHILDREN. BRING WHAT EVENING CLOTHES YOU HAVE. THE REST I'LL ATTEND TO. I NEED YOU. PLEASE COME.

She showed the wire to Bridget. Bridget

123

shook her head. "There are rumors that her husband has been playing around, but I thought they had an arrangement. However the poor child seems desperate. You must go."

"I wonder if the children's passports are in order."

"Leave them here," Bridget said calmly. "Dolores, you've been a wonderful mother. These have been four lonely years for you. I know about loneliness . . . and you've borne it like a champion. You deserve a holiday. The children are having a marvelous time with Michael and Joyce's children—and Bonnie is coming next week with her brood and Anna and Beatrice are also arriving then. We'll have more nurses than we need, and the children love it here. You go alone and have a marvelous time."

Just before she left, Bridget pressed an envelope into her hand. "Buy yourself some perfume or a nice frock."

When Dolores opened it there were two five-hundred-dollar bills.

She bought herself two new evening gowns and packed her best clothes. She also threw in some slacks and heavy sweaters. She wondered what had happened. Had Nelson found out about Erick? Had Nita taken too many pills and told him? Oh God . . . then he could toss her out . . . and it was obvious Erick hadn't taken Nita back, else there wouldn't be the cable.

The Secret Service men got her on the TWA plane before the other passengers boarded and the hostess assured her that it was a light flight and no one would sit next to her. In fact, the hostess said she'd even block off the seats across the aisle. In this way, Dolores would have complete privacy.

She ate a lot . . . watched the movie . . . but throughout the trip she wondered about Nita. What could have happened? Nita had confided to Horatio about Erick. Horatio was a gossip . . . and Erick had contacts all over the world. No, it had to be trouble with Nelson because Nelson was her bulwark . . . she didn't love him . . . but the knowledge that she was Lady Bramley and there was plenty of money behind her gave her a certain security.

When she saw Nita with Nelson on the field as the plane settled down, she felt a great wave of relief. Obviously there was nothing wrong between them. She was given courtesy of the port and her passport was inspected on the field. "The airport inside is black with cameramen and newspapermen," Nelson explained. "This way we'll be able to get away from them."

And then in a matter of minutes they were in the limousine, heading for London. Lord Bramley's man would attend to her luggage.

"It's been so long since I've been here,"

Dolores said, looking out of the windows eagerly.

"We're delighted you could come," Lord Bramley said. "I realize it's only four o'clock in the afternoon, your time, but it's nine our time. I've arranged a private supper for you and Nita so you can talk. Tomorrow you must sleep and catch up with the jet lag. The parties start the following day. And a good round of them we have, too, finalizing with a ball of our own in your honor at the country estate."

"We're staying at the flat now," Nita added. "I thought you'd like to be in London. There are some marvelous designers I want you to see, and we must fly over to Paris. Baron Erick de Savonne is putting his jet at our disposal. He's also coming to the ball for you."

"Nita likes the chap," Nelson said as he lit a cigarette. "I think he's a crashing bore— both he and his ballerina friend. But then Nita has always liked to surround herself with colorful people . . . and the Baron is colorful if nothing else. Anyone worth twenty billion *is* colorful, I must say."

"Oh, silly," Nita said lightly. "All the Rothschilds are flying in for the ball, and if Melina Mercouri and Maria Callas are here, they'll come too. I've also invited some of the young debs, and of course Regine will fly in . . . and we have more titles . . . including all the Italian royalty *moneyed* eligibles . . . Oh Dolores, it's going to be marvelous."

Dolores settled back in the car. Suddenly she understood. Nita had established contact with Erick and she wanted to give the most dazzling party in Europe. And *she*, Dolores, was the bait.

She shrank into the car when she saw the press lined up in front of the Belgravia flat. It looked like a mob scene. There were police holding them at bay but they surged forward when she got out of the car. She managed a smile, a brief wave, and when TV and radio microphones were shoved in her face, she said in a small voice, "I'm here to visit my sister. I haven't been to Europe since—" She halted and was amazed herself that tears came to her eyes, but the picture of the smiling Jimmy suddenly came to her mind. Jimmy so filled with life . . . the tears weren't because she missed him . . . but the compassion she suddenly felt that he was dead . . . lying in the ground . . . his body decomposing . . . the flesh falling off that smiling face . . . he would never see his children grown . . . he was dead . . . but life went on. She put her head down and made a dash for the flat.

21. The Proposal

THE "flat" was a town house with enormous rooms. It seemed there were servants everywhere. They actually lined up to be introduced and greet her. A young girl named Agnes was designated as her personal maid.

She had some sherry before the fire with Nelson and Nita. Then he stood up and said, "I hope you won't think it rude of me, but it is close to eleven and tomorrow is a work day. I'll leave you to catch up." He kissed Dolores lightly on the cheek, gave Nita the same kind of a kiss, and left the room.

For a moment both sisters were silent. Dolores stared at the tall ceilings, the tapestries, the English paintings. Finally Nita said, "I'm sure my cable came as a surprise."

"A nice surprise now," Dolores said. "I was frightened that something was wrong." She stretched out. "Oh Nita . . . it's so good to be here. I want to have fun . . . to go to

the theater here . . . to browse around stores.
I hear there's a wonderful designer here named
Thea Porter."

"Darling, you're too famous to ever
browse. I think the Queen of England would
have a better chance. Tomorrow your picture
will be on every front page in London. But
I'll take you to Thea's."

Nita stood up. "I imagine Agnes has you
unpacked by now. Let's go up so we can really
talk."

"Nothing is really wrong, is it?"

"The children are well. Nelson is between loves. I am not on Demerol . . . I was
for three days but I've come out of it now. I'm
fine. As they say in the States, I've got my head
together . . . and we must talk."

Dolores gasped as she entered the bedroom. It had been redone since she had last
seen it. The canopied bed . . . the fireplace
. . . the silver service . . . tea and sandwiches
were laid out on the coffee table . . . Agnes,
at attention, waiting to serve.

"I've unpacked everything, Ma'am . . .
and the bell on your night table will summon
me if there's anything you wish. I took the
liberty of taking most of your clothes to be
pressed. They'll be ready before you awaken."

"Agnes is a genius with the iron," Nita
said.

"Oh, but if you forgive me, my lady

. . . Madame traveled very very light. Only two bags and a case."

"Mrs. Ryan purposely traveled light," Nita said to the maid. "One of the main reasons she came to London is to shop here and in Paris and perhaps Rome. Now you can leave, Agnes . . . I'll pour."

"Yes, my lady . . . and Myrtle wants to know if there's anything special you'll be wanting."

"No, tell Myrtle to go to bed."

Agnes actually bowed out. "Myrtle's mine," Nita said with an attempt at a smile. "Want some tea?"

"Of course," Dolores said. "And I see you've got those marvelous cucumber sandwiches. I'm starving."

"Didn't you eat on the plane?"

"Yes, but that was hours ago. Don't forget—it's not even eight P.M. my time."

"Dolo, you could lose some weight."

Dolores bit into the sandwich and leaned back. "And you could gain some." There was a slight tap on the door. The butler entered with a cable on a tray. He handed it to Dolores. When he left, Dolores said, "This reminds me of my days at the White House. *Everything* came on a tray. In the beginning I used to feel as if I should tip them."

"Aren't you going to open your cable?"

"It's probably from Bridget telling me

the children are fine." Dolores ripped it open.
CAME BACK FOR TWO DAYS. LEARNED YOU WERE
GONE. GOING BACK TO PALM BEACH. MISS YOU
VERY VERY MUCH. LOVE. B.

She wanted to hold it close. . . . Barry
had missed her enough to send this cable.
Suddenly she was sorry she had come. To have
missed two whole days with him. She could
have found a pretext to come up from Virginia . . . a toothache . . . a loose inlay . . .
Bridget was easy to fool. She knew Nita was
watching her. She smiled.

"It's from Barclay Houseman . . . he's
that Junior Senator who's been calling me. He
came in from Washington and found I was
gone. He's a bore." She crumpled up the tele-
gram and left it on the coffee table.

Nita picked it up. "He sounds smitten.
Why does he sign it B.? And not his name?"

"Probably to protect me from gossip on
the chance that one of your staff might open it.
Really, he's only thirty-two . . . and dreary.
Those are the kind I get . . . those are the
ones who send *me* cables. No one dashing like
Robert Redford or George C. Scott."

"Do you fancy George C. Scott?" Nita
asked.

"I don't fancy anyone," Dolores answered. "I just admire their talent."

"George C. Scott is not elegant-looking,"
Nita said.

"No, he isn't. I doubt whether anyone

who has had his nose broken several times can look elegant."

"How do you know that?"

"Oh, I read it somewhere. I read a lot, Nita."

"I don't think Erick is any more gross-looking than George C. Scott."

"Nita, let's drop poor Mr. Scott. Right now he's probably in the arms of his beautiful young wife. Why are we talking about him?"

"Because I want to talk about Erick."

Dolores lit a cigarette. "That goes without saying . . . I'm waiting."

"But you think Erick is gross."

"What does it matter what I think of Erick?"

"Because he wants to marry you."

22. The Answer

DOLORES dropped her cigarette. She hastily picked it up and rubbed the spot on the rug. "It's terrible the way I can't smoke in public," she said. "The image I'm supposed to uphold . . ." She knew she was speaking gibberish but she couldn't meet the steely gaze of Nita. "Jimmy once told me I shouldn't be seen smoking in public and—"

"Shut up!" Nita hissed. "I said he wants to marry you."

"But I don't want to marry him. I don't like him."

"How can you say that? You don't really know him."

"I've met him . . . maybe three times. That was enough."

"I want you to marry him, Dolores."

"But why? I thought you loved him."

"I do. But I can never have him. I know that now. He doesn't know what love means.

Maybe he's got something for Ludmilla . . .
they've been together so long . . . she's like
an old shoe. We had an evening together . . .
that bastard. He allowed me to tell him I
couldn't live without him. He even accepted
the platinum cigarette case I gave him. Then
he patted my head and said, 'Little girl, you
don't love me. It's my power and my money
you love. But you do have something I want.'
Dolo . . . I leaned forward . . . willing to
settle on any terms . . . then he said, 'I want
to marry your sister.' I actually burst into tears.
But he calmed me down and he said, 'I know
money is not an urgency to you, because your
husband has money. He has exactly six hundred thousand pounds plus his estates. But you
do not love him and you must stay with him
when he wishes and appear when he summons
and close your eyes to his blatant affairs, because you yourself have no money. But I will
give you five million dollars if you get your
sister to marry me.'"

"But why? I mean . . . we've rarely
talked . . ."

Nita shook her head. "I don't know. But
don't dismiss the idea, Dolo. After all, what
kind of a life do you lead in New York . . .
or anywhere? You sit alone night after night,
go for long walks with the kids, lunch with
Bridget, make the Best Dressed List with my
hand-me-downs. You go to maybe six functions
a year with Michael or that Judge. Then

there're those glorious holidays at the farm
. . . summers in Newport . . ."

"But I couldn't allow him to touch me.
I can't stand him." Dolores actually shivered.

"Dolo, he is a great lover . . . gentle
. . . considerate . . . and at sixty-two, he has
more virility than any man alive. We had one
last night of sex together . . . *before* he made
this little proposition. Dolo . . . think . . .
think what a marvelous life it would be for
you. You'd have all the money you could ever
spend . . . that ocean liner would be yours
. . . you'd have your own plane . . . it would
be like life at the White House . . . only
greater . . . because he wouldn't be nagging
at you on what you spent. He told me . . .
he'd give you the world . . . plus an enormous
marriage contract."

"Marriage contract?"

"He has four sons. If he left a great mass
of money to you in a will, they might sue to
break it. You'd spend years in litigation. He
said he would settle five million on you, tax-
free, when you married. And in the event *you*
divorce him, and it's agreeable to him, you'd
keep the five million, plus get an additional five
million as the divorce settlement. The worst
that could happen would be if you married
him . . . and eventually agreed on an ami-
cable divorce, you'd be worth ten million, plus
all the jewels. And if you stayed together,
you'd have your own five million, plus a life

style beyond anything you could imagine. Dolo, you'd have everything . . . anything you ever wanted."

"Except love."

"You haven't had love for years. In fact, I don't think you've ever had love. Jimmy cheated on you all the time. Not only did the Secret Service turn their faces the other way when his friends smuggled obliging quickies into his hotel suites on all those trips he made, but they were also slipping hookers through the back door at 1600 Pennsylvania Avenue. You never really loved him. And Dolo . . . I'd have five million and I could walk out on that sonofabitch I'm married to. And maybe I'd find someone else. A woman with five million dollars can find plenty of divine lovers."

Dolores shook her head. She refrained from looking at the crumpled cable. "I'm sorry, Nita. The answer is No!"

23. Furs

SHE remained throughout the Easter holidays. Nita kept at her, but she remained adamant. Sometimes Nita pleaded, other times she threatened. "I'll never send you another outfit again or lend you money when you run short." Dolores merely remained stoically silent.

There were the parties, climaxed by the huge ball Nita and Lord Bramley gave for her. The Baron arrived without Ludmilla. He danced with Dolores several times. He was tall, well-built, but he looked sixty-two—and she was thirty-nine and insanely in love with Barry. She noticed he smelled of clean soap and there *was* an overpowering masculinity about him. As a friend she might like him. As an escort he would be wonderful. But as a husband . . . she looked at his large hands . . . even to think of them touching her body made her shudder.

It was after the third dance that he

looked down at her with a smile and said, "You reject my offer, I hear."

"I'm not in the habit of getting marriage proposals without love. And also through another person."

"Odd to me that you are not a good business person. I always thought that Americans had the big talent to make money."

"That's usually separated from marriage in America. At least we choose to think that love and marriage are part of the American Dream." Then she laughed lightly. "Of course if there happens to be sufficient money, then that's all the better."

"And you . . . what about your money?"

"Sufficient."

"I know otherwise. Not only from your sister, but from many sources whom I had investigate you. How can a beautiful woman, with three children, live on thirty thousand a year? I would give you more than that in one day to spend on furs."

"When and how did you fall in love with me?"

"Who said anything about love?"

She stood off a bit as they danced and studied him. "Then why do you want to marry me?"

"I have my reasons . . . just as I felt you might have your reasons for marrying me."

"My reasons would be the unlimited

money you'd give me?" He nodded and she went on. "But why would you choose me?"

"I want to be President of France one day."

She gasped. The way he had stated it . . . cold and businesslike. Not even an attempt to say she attracted him. She knew people were watching them so she managed a smile. "And by marrying me, you think you could achieve this?"

"I have been married once. Divorced once. Married again. Then my wife died. But for years I have had a mistress. It has been a highly publicized affair because my mistress has great beauty and talent. But marriage to you would give me a new image. The beloved widow of the most popular American President, marrying Baron Erick de Savonne—it would electrify the world. The public has you on a pedestal. They think of me as machismo, a man with many women passing through his life and one tempestuous mistress. But all the women would be wiped from the public's eye if I married the most important, most respected woman in the world."

She managed a light laugh. "I realize being President of France is an ultimate aim for you. But I've been a President's wife before."

"But have you ever had all the money in the world to spend? Your own personal ocean liner . . . villas everywhere . . . a free

rein to entertain as lavishly as you wish . . .
jewels that you cannot imagine . . . homes to
decorate as you wish . . . galas to throw . . .
European royalty as your friends? I know it is
true that you met all those people as the wife
of an American President, but that is gone
now. For the past few years—your most magnificent years—you have been vegetating."

She smiled. "You have forgotten one important thing."

"You are not going to speak of love
again. You sound like a schoolgirl."

"No, I'm speaking of my religion. I am
Catholic. I am not the best Catholic in the
world, but my religion does help me and I believe in it. I am raising my children as Catholics. Even if I wanted to marry you . . . it
would be impossible. You are a divorced man."

"I could have that marriage annulled."

"With four sons . . ."

"I can do anything."

"Except buy me. . . . And I think I'm
a bit tired now. I'd like to stop dancing."

24. The Happiest Woman in the World

SHE spent three lonely nights back in the States. The children were back in school, but Constance had lured Barry into a trip on a friend's yacht. He came back a week later, tanned and more handsome than ever. She could hardly keep from throwing herself in his arms, but Mary Lou and the twins were hugging him and calling him Uncle Barry.

Finally they were alone. She barely ate the dinner that the cook had prepared . . . he seemed hungry . . . but when the meal was over and the house was asleep she rushed into his arms. And that night they were closer than ever. Later as they were having a cigarette, she lay back and studied his handsome profile and shuddered as she thought of Erick. For the first time in her life she knew what love was really about . . . she loved someone more than herself . . . she wanted to please Barry . . . she wanted to be with Barry . . . nothing else mattered.

Suddenly he got up and began dressing.
"Where are you going? It's almost midnight."

"Home."

She leaped out of bed and clung to him.
"Barry, have I done something wrong? Have
I been too demanding? It's just that we've been
separated for four weeks and—"

He held her close and stroked her hair.
"You've done nothing wrong. I love you. I've
thought of you every second of the four weeks.
I've thought of you during the endless cocktail
parties with the same faces . . . the talk of
backgammon, tennis . . . all I saw was you
. . . and your children. I'll never have any
children now. Constance is beginning to go
through the change . . . she's not feeling too
well. One day it's hot flashes . . . the next day
her heart is pounding . . . the doctor told her
it was just the change but she won't accept it.
She refuses to believe this is happening, so she
came back with me. She wants to see some
specialists. That's why I have to go home. She
thinks this is poker night."

"Oh, I thought she'd stay in Palm Beach
through April."

Barry nodded as he dressed. "She usually does. But this time she insists on going to
her New York doctor who will tell her the
same thing. And then she'll go to the hospital
for a checkup. She's really playing Camille."

"Then I won't see you till—"

"Tomorrow for a drink. But Wednesday, I'll tell her it's a board meeting and a late dinner with some members of the firm."

"I love you, Barry." She slipped into a robe and walked him to the door. Suddenly she clung to him. "I feel so alone without you. I have nobody . . ."

"Dolores, you have many people."

"I never really had anyone. I wasn't close to my mother, and she's gone now. I wasn't close to Nita. I thought we had grown close while she was here, but I don't like the people she goes with. I have my children, but they are like all children—to them I represent a trip to the zoo . . . help with their French lessons . . . someone to listen to their prayers . . . along with an occasional outing to the park or museums. But Mary Lou is already much more interested in her girlfriends—goes for 'sleepovers'—and the twins are occupied with each other." She laughed lightly. "So you see, Barry—you are the only person in my life."

"You sell people too short," he said. "There's a whole world out there that would give anything to know you and love you."

She laughed aloud. "And what do I do? Go out with a sign saying, 'good, healthy, slightly used President's widow looking for companionship'?"

He laughed, too. "You're like Greta Garbo, my love, closed in with invisible silken walls, for all the world to worship—or at least

that was the way I thought about her twenty
years ago and when I met her I found she had
a great sense of humor and was very outgoing.
God, think of all the fun she missed."

"Maybe she missed nothing. She might
have had a Barry Haines in her life. Right now,
with you holding me, I think I'm the happiest
woman in the world. I don't need anyone else."

25. The Yacht

BARRY didn't arrive the following day for cocktails. His call came at seven. "Darling, there was no way of reaching you before this. I'm in a booth now at Doctors Hospital."

"What's wrong?"

"Nothing. Connie's doctor checked her out and told her it was the beginning of the menopause, and she refused to accept it. She's here with *three* doctors, to give her every test. I suggested she go to Mayo, but she likes it here. I can come over at ten if it's not too late. They throw me out of here then."

"I'll have dinner waiting."

"No, I'll eat here. You can order room service here. See you at ten."

They had five wonderful nights together . . . but when he arrived on the sixth day at cocktail time, she knew something was wrong the moment he walked in.

"Sit down, Barry. What is it?"

"Constance!"

"She's found out about us?"

"No, she has something wrong. The tests finally came through. High blood pressure and diabetes."

She sighed in relief. "Oh that . . . I mean . . . it's dreadful . . . but it can be kept under control and she can live a long life."

"It's the needles that bug her. The doctors say that oral insulin is not for her . . . not now anyway . . . her sugar content is too high. And of course the high blood pressure bothers her. She's always played golf and been active. She thinks it will make her a semi-invalid."

"But that's not true! Oh, she might have to take things easy for a few months, but she'll live a long life."

"You just said it all."

"I don't understand."

"She'll live a long, frightened, inactive life. She'll be discharged from the hospital tomorrow. And she's already hired a nurse who will give her shots and 'borrowed' Debbie Morrow's yacht. She wants a month of rest and she loves the water."

"But that's marvelous."

"It's not marvelous. She insists that I go with her."

Dolores tried to hold back the tears.

Barry paced the room. "She's even talked with the head of my law firm. They insist I go with her. There's no way out. It's so ridiculous. As you said, diabetes isn't something you look forward to . . . but it's not cancer. And high blood pressure can be controlled. But I guess it's because she's always been so healthy that she's frightened. Dolores, I have to go with her."

"A month," Dolores said quietly.

"An age . . ." he said.

She clung to him. "You've got to go, Barry. I understand. And a month isn't forever. Look, when you get back, the trees will be green . . . it will be May . . . we'll have May together in New York . . ." She turned away. She didn't want him to see the tears in her eyes.

He walked to the door. She turned and rushed after him. "She's still in the hospital. Can't you stay tonight?"

"No, I've got to have dinner with her. Then I've got to pack and see to it that her maid packs for her . . . she wants to leave tomorrow."

"Tomorrow! Is she well enough?"

"The doctors recommend it. They don't want her to get mentally depressed too. And she *is* going through the change. So we leave for Palm Beach where the boat is docked tomorrow."

"Try and write."

"I'll do better. I'll phone from every port we stop at . . . I hope Debbie comes

along. That will take some of the pressure off
me."

"Debbie?"

"Debbie Morrow, the woman who owns
the boat."

Dolores managed a smile. "I know Debbie. She must be fifty-five. It sounds funny for
a woman that age to be called by such a child-
ish name."

"Debbie also has over fifty million and
it's her yacht and it's called *Debbie,* too. I
guess when you have that kind of money you
can be called Debbie until you're ninety if you
want it that way."

"Where did Debbie get her money?"

"It's old money, darling . . . and she
married old money and he died and left her
even more." Suddenly he grabbed her. "Why
are two beautiful people like us poor?"

"Because Debbie and Constance *need*
their money . . . we just need each other."

26. That Certain Something

HE called at least once a week but her loneliness without him was almost unbearable. She took bike rides in the park with the children and the Secret Service men. Photographers were always parked outside the River View House. She pretended to ignore them, but she didn't mind. Her publicity had been flagging lately . . . she had made the cover of only one movie magazine this month . . . an opening at Lincoln Center she had been to with Michael (Eddie Harris was going with a new young English superstar). And Michael had said Joyce was beginning to kick about his trips to New York, making odd accusations. That night he had come back to her apartment to talk to her.

"I want to take you to the opening of *Hattie* tomorrow night," he said as he poured himself a brandy.

She stared out at the East River. "We'll

make all the newspapers and you said Joyce was beginning to kick about all your trips to New York."

"Oh, she doesn't worry about you. Funny . . . Joyce is the complete opposite of you in looks. I mean she's tiny . . . outgoing . . . gregarious. She's into every charity . . . has unbelievable energy . . . yet she considers you no rival."

"Then what is it?"

"She senses something. She's very intuitive."

Dolores turned her back and fiddled with the air conditioner. "It is warm in here. Why is it they never start the air conditioning until the middle of May? This has been an unseasonably hot April." She was stalling for time. Michael was very handsome, but he was totally void of sex appeal as far as she was concerned. But she needed Michael. She needed him to take her out occasionally. Eddie Harris was gone now . . . the Supreme Court Judge was so dreary and she no longer made news with him . . . but she knew there were murmurs about her and Michael and as dull as he was, God, he was handsome and they looked so brilliant together. And as long as there were rumors about her and Michael it would throw everyone off the track about Barry. Barry! Just thinking about him made her feel almost lightheaded. He'd be back in less than ten days . . . to feel his arms around her . . . to kiss him deeply . . . the way she had never really been able to kiss Jimmy or any man . . . did people realize a deep kiss could be closer than actual intercourse?

"Dolores, stop trying to make the air conditioner work. I'll open the windows if you like, but it's really quite pleasant in here."

She turned and looked at Michael. He was sitting in Barry's favorite chair. If she had to go to bed with him occasionally to hold him . . . No! She couldn't.

"Dolores, will you settle down. I want to talk to you."

"I've got to go in and see if the children are all right."

"For God's sake, they're not babies. It's not as if you have to 'turn' them in a crib. Mary Lou is enormous and the twins are strapping young boys."

She sat on the edge of the couch. "I don't think we should go to the opening of *Hattie* tomorrow. It's going to be a tremendous opening. June Ames has already had sensational publicity. She's broken every rule. That seems to be the consensus of all the press. I mean, when you're one of the most beautiful young movie stars and a big box office attraction, you don't take chances doing a Broadway musical, do you? One of the newscasters on TV did a big story on this just the other night. You know . . . the idea that she has everything to lose, and nothing to gain. She'll never convince the critics that she's anything more than just a beautiful face."

"Why are you rambling on like this when you know I want to talk to you?" He was visibly annoyed. "I want to talk to you about something serious. And how come you are so well informed about the career of June Ames?"

"I read all the fan magazines to keep up with my own publicity," she said impishly. "And I do listen to television and read all the newspapers. There isn't very much else I can do to fill my time."

"What about girlfriends? Joyce has loads of them. And charities?"

"Joyce is a Senator's wife and lives in Washington. I am—"

"Queen Victoria. Only a beautiful one."

"Well, you've got to say that all the newspapers call me mysterious, beautiful, charismatic . . ."

He stared at her for a moment. "I think you actually believe all the junk that's written about you."

"I wish I did," she said slowly.

"You are beautiful."

"Nita is far more beautiful."

"Yes, she is. And I'm better-looking than Jimmy. But he had that certain something that turned people on. Even when we were both in the Senate together . . . when he stood up . . . he had a presence. And you've got it, too. Nita hasn't."

"Look, Michael . . ." She knew he was about to confess his love for her and somehow she had to stop him. "We can't go to *Hattie* together. You know as well as I do there are slight innuendos about us . . . nothing could be further from the truth . . . but if we appeared together . . . two nights in a row . . ."

"That's just it! I want them to think that . . . I want Joyce to think that . . ."

"Are you mad?"

"No . . . I have my reasons."

"Don't you think you ought to tell me?"

He looked down at the floor. "Okay," he said quietly. "For two years I've been having an affair with June Ames."

For a moment Dolores couldn't speak. The whole thing was so incredible.

"Why do you think I make it a point to be seen with you at least once a month? You're my red herring. I've just put our oldest son into military school in Connecticut so I'll always have that as an excuse to come here. And a guy I went to school with is co-producer of *Hattie* . . . Colin Wright. I put up twenty-five thousand dollars in a corporate name. Joyce knows I'm friendly with Colin. We've had him to the house before, when he had shows trying out in Washington. So Colin will always beard for us if June and I are seen in public . . . and I've always got you once a month . . . and if I come here and am seen with Colin, Joyce won't have a glimmer or even put up an argu-

ment. Just as long as I'm not with you. She'll
raise hell after tomorrow about you if we go
to see *Hattie* together."

"Only we're not going to see *Hattie* together," she said sweetly.

He stood up and grabbed her by the
shoulders. "You cold bitch. You've never loved
anyone but yourself. You never loved my
brother. I was crazy to tell you this . . . to ex-
pect you to understand. When Jimmy used to
tell me about his extracurricular interests, I'd
give him hell . . . tell him how beautiful you
were . . . and he'd say, 'But Mike, she just
tolerates me in bed!' Well, now I believe him.
You wouldn't know what it is to love . . . to
physically long for someone. The trips I've
made to the Coast . . . thank God my sister is
married to a doctor out there and the marriage
is rocky. I've used that as an excuse to go out
there. You're damned right that June has placed
her career on the line. And do you know why?
Because she loves me. She loves me enough to
take a chance with that brilliant career even
though she knows there's no chance of a divorce. But she's playing the long shot that the
show will make it and this way there won't be
three thousand miles between us. I'll be able
to come in every week. I can even fly in on the
shuttle for the day . . . and get back in time
for dinner with Joyce. I'd do that . . . but you
wouldn't understand that kind of love. You'd

think it was cheap. Without a wedding ring, there is no such thing as love with you."

"Michael—" she broke away from him. "I do understand how you feel. And if you and this girl find some kind of happiness together it's wonderful . . . as long as no one else is hurt. But you are tossing me to the lions to make this affair less complicated. Not only will Joyce hate me . . . but the press will make veiled remarks. My children go to school . . . they'll hear things other children will repeat that they hear from their mothers . . ."

"Dolores, if you just go tomorrow night, I'll never ask you for another favor."

"What about Joyce? How come she's not eager to come in for the opening?"

"She saw it with me when it tried out in Washington. She even came back and met June, and the four of us—Colin, June and Joyce and I—had supper together. It made all the Washington papers. People think Colin and June are having a romance. Joyce bought it."

"How does Colin feel about being the beard?"

"He adores it. He's gay . . . lives with a set designer . . . loves the image of a sex queen like June being 'in love' with him. And they're good friends."

"What makes you think Joyce won't come in when you visit your son at school?"

"Because she's four months pregnant and

she lost the last one. The doctor told her she needs a lot of bed rest."

"You've got everything planned, haven't you?"

"Everything except the notices. They could be rotten. It would kill June . . . then she'd go back to the Coast . . ."

"Is it a good show?"

He shrugged. "I can't tell. I love her so much that just seeing her on stage makes me feel good. It got mixed notices in Washington, but they did a lot of work and then played three weeks in Philadelphia, where the notices were fairly good. Poor Junie. She'd be playing a show at night, rehearsing new scenes and new songs during the day, putting them in that night. And she's not eighteen!"

"How old is she . . . really?"

"Twenty-seven for the press . . . actually she's thirty. But she looks twenty-four."

Dolores stared at the floor. "You really love her, don't you?"

"Yes I do, Dolores."

"Would you give up your religion and get a divorce for her?"

"I'd give up everything for her. But Joyce would never divorce me . . . never. She's like Bridget. They go to Mass together almost every day. I mean . . . they believe in it all."

"Don't you?"

"I do . . . but I don't think God would

turn me out if I became an Episcopalian. I think he'd turn me out only if I broke Joyce's heart and hurt the kids . . . and that's what divorce would do."

She smiled faintly. "All right, Michael . . . I'll go to *Hattie* with you tomorrow night."

27. Notices

SHE went to Donald Brooks and he created a gown for her . . . made it up that very day. She knew she would get worldwide press on this and she had to look her best. He also made her a fantastic coat to go with it . . . actually he didn't make it . . . it was his newest model . . . yet to be shown. And he had the neckline raised . . . and the sleeves adjusted . . . the shoulders of the coat changed . . . fur added to the hem of the coat. "If you lost about ten pounds, I could lend you all my model clothes," he said.

"Am I fat?" she asked.

"No . . . but you're not model-thin."

That night she weighed herself. One hundred and twenty-eight! She had gained three pounds. But her figure was in proportion . . . her breasts solid . . . her stomach flat . . . it was well distributed . . . and there wasn't a line in her face.

She knew she had never looked as beautiful before. Even Michael gasped when he arrived to pick her up. The hairdresser had worked three hours with a new hairpiece . . . no one could detect it . . . no one ever had . . . the newspapers always talked about her "lion's mane" . . . and she looked like a lioness tonight. She had used a tan makeup . . . a bronze lipstick . . . and the dress was golden beige trimmed with sable.

There was a roar when her car pulled up to the theater. The police whistled for added help . . . the fans screamed . . . the news cameras followed her to her seat. The entire theater was filled with celebrities and well-known first nighters. But Dolores got all the attention.

At intermission the police came to escort her to the manager's office. She and Michael had a drink there. Colin popped in and asked everyone how they thought it was going. Everyone seemed hysterically enthusiastic.

The police arrived at her seat right before the final curtain and she and Michael ducked down the aisle while the cast was taking the numerous curtain calls. June was taking her fifth solo bow and calling the rest of the cast back to the stage when the manager led Michael and Dolores backstage through a door inside the theater.

They were in the wings as the cast came

off. Everyone looked slightly grotesque and fatigued under the heavy makeup. They stopped riveted to the spot when they saw Dolores. She smiled graciously. June came forward and Colin presented her. Dolores stood like royalty and shook hands with every member of the cast.

Then Colin led them to a suite that served as a dressing room for June. She had already taken off all her makeup and Dolores was amazed how beautiful she was "barefaced." There was a small TV set in the sitting room and the maid pointed toward a makeshift bar. Colin mixed martinis. "I know Michael and I go for this. June likes vodka and water. What is your preference, Mrs. Ryan?"

"A light Scotch and water."

"Listen," Colin went on. "We've taken the upstairs room at Sardi's for a cast party." He clicked on the TV screen. "The notices will be coming in any second."

"I thought only the *Times* meant anything," Dolores said.

"Oh, that's the big Daddy, but TV helps. I mean the good critics, not haters and smirkers like that runt on Channel Five. You'd be surprised . . . but the public gets on to them. They say, 'Oh, *they* hate everything, so I'll see for myself.' But the good TV critics *can* help. So can the columnists. But with a rave in the *Times,* you're in!"

"I'll take Dolores home. Do you think it's safe now . . . I mean, has the crowd left?" Michael asked.

Dolores almost dropped her drink. She was looking forward to the party at Sardi's.

"Half of the hard core autograph hunters will have already taken their post at Sardi's, to get the celebrities who are coming in. But the press will be watching your limousine."

"Well, let's brave it," Michael said as he finished his drink. "I'll take Dolores home . . . have the limo take me to the hotel . . . shake the press that way. Then I'll slip out and go by foot to Sardi's."

"The press will know you've come to the party," Colin warned. "Maybe if Dolores didn't mind . . . and came for a short time . . ."

"Oh, I wouldn't put her through that," Michael said. "Besides, I can always say that I came back on impulse to sit with my college buddy, Colin Wright, to wait for the notices. They'll buy that." He stood up and walked over to June. "I'll see you over there, darling. I know you'll get rave reviews, but no matter what they say, I want you to know you were magnificent."

Dolores saw the girl look into his eyes. And suddenly her heart went out to her, because she could see June Ames really loved Michael and she had no future . . . just as she and Barry were doomed.

She ignored the crowd that almost halted their car and was very silent on the drive across town.

"You disapprove," Michael finally said.

"Only because the girl is going to be hurt."

"I love her, Dolores."

"I don't doubt that. But what happens to her? She really loves you. As you said . . . she's thirty. I believe she was divorced."

"A childhood marriage. She was seventeen and singing with a local band in Texas and she married the drummer."

"All right. She's not a real actress. I mean she won't last like say a Joan Crawford or Barbara Stanwyck—these women were all beautiful glamour girls, but they had something to back it up. Your June is candy-box pretty but she won't grow into an exciting-looking woman in her forties. She'll be faded, and you'll tire of her . . . and her career will go down the drain."

"Good God, we've gone together for two years. Our love is stronger than ever. Who wants to plan on ten years from now? That's what you probably did with Jimmy. I know what you're like—everything is categorized. Eight years at the White House . . . then perhaps Jimmy would head a legal firm . . . a big social life in New York or Washington. But it didn't work out that way, did it? Jimmy was killed. You've lived like a hermit for several years. And now what have you planned? To become a legend? Well, if that gives you any satisfaction . . . you are. Does that make you happy when you climb into your virginal bed? Do all the photographs in newspapers and on magazine covers make up for the lack of any emotion in your life? Emotions you've never tapped or never known—"

"You know so little about me," she said quietly.

"I know you like I know my right hand." They had pulled up before her apartment. He got out of the car, and took her to the elevator.

"Michael, you don't have to see me up."

"It will only take a minute," he said as he pressed for the elevator. "Listen, Dolores, marry the Chief Justice. He's old enough not to bother you with sex. He has a lovely house in Georgetown, a farm in Chevy Chase, an apartment here, and . . ." He pressed the elevator button impatiently. "Where the hell is that elevator man?"

"He's probably delivering papers on each floor." She looked up. "He's coming down now. Michael, try not to hurt that little actress."

"I love her."

She smiled mistily as the elevator arrived. "I hope the show runs forever. Have a wonderful night tonight. Please, don't bother coming up." She looked at her watch. "The notices will be coming out any minute. She'll need you if they're bad and she'll want to share them with you if they're good."

He stared at her oddly. "Dolores, no wonder you're talked about as the most complex woman in the world. Suddenly I don't feel I know you all that well. . . ." Then he turned and hurried back to his car.

28. Soap and Water

THE notices had been excellent, and she saw Michael occasionally. Once they went to the opera (while June was doing her own show), and, with Colin along, they all went to Sardi's.

And on the fifteenth of May, Barry returned. He rushed to her apartment, tanned and as handsome as ever. For the first time he completely disregarded the children and grabbed her . . . kissed her and said, "Oh God, how I've missed you." And then he was hugging the twins and kissing a suddenly shy Mary Lou. "You've grown," he told her. "Soon you'll be as tall as Mommy."

"Will I be as pretty as Mommy?"

"Prettier," he said.

And that night they lay locked in one another's arms as if they had never been apart. "Can you stay the night?" she whispered.

"No . . . this is a 'board meeting' night."

"Will she go to the country June fifteenth as usual?"

"Yes . . . and then we'll have five days and nights together for three months. Just weekends apart."

"All right. Then I'll send the twins to camp also."

"What do you mean?"

"Well, Mary Lou is all set for camp in Maine. I was going to keep the twins with me and go to Virginia with them on weekends . . . and leave them there most of the summer. But this time I'll send them to camp. Then I'll have no obligations. I'll be completely free for you. And I'll visit Bridget on weekends."

He kissed her gently. "I love you so much, Dolores."

"Not as much as I love you," she said.

He rolled over and lit a cigarette. "I feel as if we're entitled to this love. I spent five hellish weeks with Constance and Debbie, watching them play backgammon, going to bed early with Constance . . . Oh, no sex. In the past we only had that twice a month when her charts said she was most likely to conceive. But thank God all that's over. She's terrified it might raise her blood pressure. But the trip was murder. All I had for company was some gay Muscle Beach athlete Debbie had along. I'd get wiped out each morning just watching him do twenty minutes of pushups. He's twenty-eight and confided in me that he wants to marry her."

"Do you think she will?"

He ground out his cigarette. "Debbie's too smart. She'll be fifty-six next month and she has enough money to buy herself handsome gay guys or not too gay guys until she's a hundred and six."

"She looks very well for her age."

"Why shouldn't she? Constance told me she's had everything lifted. I've got to give Constance credit . . . her figure is still good and until her illness she worked at it. Twenty minutes a day of yoga . . . no carbohydrates. She's gained a few pounds now and she's worried sick. In fact she's going to ask her doctor whether she can have some 'lifts' in her condition."

Dolores stretched in bed. His body was so firm. "Do you think I need it?"

He laughed. "You're a child."

"I'm thirty-nine . . ."

"Well, Constance will be fifty, and even she gets by with a good facial and the proper makeup. But you'd better start going easy on the sun tanning bit."

"What do you mean?"

"Well, Constance has great skin because she never gets near the sun. And you're a sun worshiper. Debbie also stays out of the sun.

She says most of those Palm Beach women look like mahogany prunes. And you know something . . . they do. Once a woman gets in her forties and keeps up that deep tan it does something to her skin."

"Is that what I look like to you—a mahogany prune?"

"You look like my golden tigress. But the next ten years is when the danger starts. So go easy on the sun. I want you to be this beautiful always."

"I'll get a face-lift tomorrow."

He laughed as he started to dress. "They can't lift sun-dried skin."

"Since when have you become such an expert?" she asked.

He laughed. "I could write a book on the care of the skin and body after forty. That's all I heard on the yacht for five weeks. Even Nature Boy rubbed himself down with a concoction of oil before he took his sun baths. And he didn't just lie in the sun . . . oh no . . . twenty minutes on one side . . . twenty on the other . . . then a glass of milk . . ."

"Milk?"

"He claims the sun gives the body a certain acidity and the milk alkalizes it. Want to hear any more of this fascinating small talk? I heard it throughout the day and with every meal. Oh, and the newest fad is to have an exercise man come in . . . he pulls your legs and you're supposed to fight him."

Dolores laughed. "Good Lord, and all I've been doing is using soap and water, riding a bike, and taking long walks."

"Good girl!" He was dressed now and she lay naked under the sheets. He had turned on the lights and for the first time she was afraid to get out of bed. Had her thighs gotten loose? Was her rear sagging a bit? He let himself out after kissing her and telling her he would come by for a drink the following day. The moment he was gone she leaped out of bed and ran into the bathroom. There was a full-length three-way mirror there. She turned on all the lights and studied herself. Her breasts were firm. Thighs good . . . very faint stretch marks . . . you had to really look to find them. She turned around . . . her fanny was getting a little loose . . . had it dropped . . . or was it her imagination?

29. Free

THE next day she went to Elizabeth Arden's; had a facial and bought a hundred dollars' worth of special creams and facial packs. Then she called a well-known exercise class and asked if a teacher would come to her home each morning.

She kept at it for ten days. She exercised frenetically, her face and body oiled with a special cream, covered with a heavy leotard that was also supposed to melt away any excess bulges. At the end of two weeks she had lost one half a pound . . . her fanny looked the same and her skin hadn't turned to velvet. She discharged the exercise man and forgot about the cream.

She allowed herself to get tan every weekend when she visited Bridget, but she no longer lay in it for hours with oil on her face. And she spent every night during the week with Barry.

And then one night in August he didn't
appear. She waited with dinner . . . no call
. . . nothing. At midnight he finally phoned.
"Dolores . . . I'm sorry . . . I couldn't get
to you until now. Constance had a stroke. I'm
at the hospital now . . . in a phone booth."

"Oh God, how is she?"

"Touch and go. It's her right side. At
the moment she's completely paralyzed and
has no speech. The doctors say with physical
therapy she has an excellent chance of a complete recovery. She'll also need speech therapy.
It's going to be a long haul, but they say her
age is all for her. Most people who get strokes
are in their sixties or seventies. I'm going to
sleep in a room adjoining hers at the hospital.
I'll call you tomorrow."

She was just falling asleep when he
called again. "She's dead," he said quietly.

"Oh Barry . . . how . . . when?"

"Ten minutes ago . . . a massive cere-
bral hemorrhage. Look . . . I'm in the phone
booth and I see her sisters getting off the elevator. Her brother is already here. I'll call you
when I get the chance."

"Barry . . . don't worry about me. I'll
be here . . . waiting."

"Oh God, Debbie Morrow just arrived
with her latest young man. I'd better go." The
receiver clicked in her ear.

She didn't hear from him for three days.
Constance's death made big news. The funeral

made all the TV news shows due to the society people who were Constance's friends and the top government officials who came in deference to Barry. Dolores sent flowers but felt it would be hypocritical to go. She sat home close to the phone and waited.

He arrived unannounced at her apartment two days after the funeral.

"Barry!" She held him close. "What you must have been through. Can I get you a drink?"

"Make me a stiff vodka martini . . . straight up." He sat down and ran his hands through his hair. "Oh God . . . funerals are barbaric. And courtesy calls even worse. All of my father's friends came. All of *her* friends came and drank. Debbie presided as if it were a giant marathon cocktail party. I even got a condolence wire from the President."

(They were free to marry now—after a respectable time—but she knew it wouldn't be wise to say anything.)

He swallowed half his drink in one gulp. "That bitch . . . that dirty evil bitch."

"Barry!"

"I've just come from the lawyer's office," he said. "Do you know what? All the time we were married, she was secretly giving her millions to her sisters . . . to endowments . . . to charities . . . setting up trusts for her sisters' children. Because she didn't have children and was older than I, she felt if she died

177

first, I'd marry some cupcake. Of course since
her first bout with high blood pressure, she
went into double action. She even willed her
jewelry to her grandnieces."

"And what about you?"

"Oh I'm in great shape!" His voice was
heavy with sarcasm. He lit a cigarette and
held out his empty glass for a refill.

"Well, legally she can't cut you out,"
Dolores said as she mixed another drink.

"Oh no. She had expert advice. I get
twenty-five thousand a year—which I pay taxes
on. I'm free to live in all the residences . . .
and the estate will take care of the help, pay
the taxes, etcetera . . . *and* . . . oh this is
the real generous part . . . if I'm alive and
unmarried at the age of sixty-five, I inherit five
million dollars. But if I'm married—nothing!"

"Is that legal?"

He nodded. "I signed some kind of a
paper when I married her. Oh the rich—the
very rich—always make you sign papers. It
seems it stated all of this . . . but good God,
I was thirty-five then and she was forty-one.
I had no money. I knew I'd never make it or
stay at the law firm on my own. The glamour
of my father's name was beginning to fade. I
was well educated to do *nothing!* So I signed
it. Constance was attractive enough . . . I
had had plenty of affairs . . . who ever figured I'd fall in love with you!"

He took the drink she handed him. He

sipped it and shook his head like a man emerging from the water. She sat at his feet and sipped at a weak Scotch. Her head had to be clear.

"Look, Barry, I don't need this large apartment. If I spoke to Bridget and explained how I felt about you, I'm sure she'd let me sell it and keep the money. It would bring in four hundred thousand dollars easily. I'm sure you could hold your law position . . . especially if you married me. Our names together would be quite glamorous. We could get a smaller apartment, perhaps on Park Avenue, and with my thirty and your twenty thousand . . . I'm sure we could manage."

He seemed to be thinking about it as he sipped his drink. "I don't know whether it would be all that easy," he said. "Don't forget, as a married couple we'd have to entertain. Part of my asset to the law firm was the excellent dinner parties Constance gave with just the right people who might be new clients." He shook his head. "No . . . we could never swing it on fifty thousand a year. Don't forget, I'd lose the extra twenty-five she's left me, and I still have to pay taxes on my twenty thousand."

"But I'd have the extra four hundred thousand from this apartment . . ."

"And how long would that last? We're not exactly going to erect a tent on Park Avenue. We'd still have to find a decent apartment, and even a smaller place in the right location would cost a hundred thousand, and we'd have to have a cook, a chauffeur, maid, nurse for the children . . . no, it couldn't work."

"Don't you think with my name I could bring you many new clients?"

"Perhaps. But once you became too public, your glamour would end."

"What do you mean?"

"Dolores, everyone talks about you because they *don't* see you around. They speculate about you . . . what is she *really* like? At the moment, getting you to attend a dinner party would be a hostess's biggest triumph. But once you started playing hostess . . . attending dinner parties with me . . . going to the country club . . . in one year, the mystique and glamour would go. You'd just be Dolores Haines. Look . . . I know. When Dad died, the Haines name had great weight. One of my brothers became Governor just because of the name. He also married a very rich woman because he didn't get elected for the second term. I was offered everything in the beginning. I knew all the offers were because of the Haines name . . . and what business that name might bring to the company. I also could have had my share of debutantes. But I found out that the ones I liked—the beautiful ones— were penniless. The rich beautiful ones went to Europe to find titles. It's incredible to think that's still being done. But it is. And then I met Constance, and I knew that with Constance I could live in style and hold my job at the law firm. If I lose it now, I'll still have the twenty-five thousand a year from her estate. That is, if I'm *not* married."

She smiled weakly. Then she slid into his lap. "Look, the world hasn't come to an end. We still have one another . . . and now we can go out publicly."

"Not for a year."

"A year!"

"That's supposed to be the proper mourning period, isn't it? Oh, I can go out with men, or attend a dinner party alone given by some of Constance's friends, but the first time you and I go out publicly . . . it will be an event."

"All right. Today is August twentieth. Next August twentieth, we'll go to Marbella together. And by then I'll find a friend who has a yacht. We can also visit Nita . . . we can have a marvelous summer. And meanwhile, for the coming year we'll just go along as we've been doing in the past. And I'll wait until you're sixty-five and inherit your money and then we'll get a priest to make the whole union respectable."

30. He Likes
His Women Thin

IN some ways it was a wonderful year. She managed to have Bridget invite Barry to the farm for Thanksgiving dinner, explaining that he was lonely and that it would be a nice gesture. "Also . . . the twins adore him. They're getting to the age where they need to see a man . . . to roughhouse with . . . to talk with . . . I . . . I've invited him to the apartment for drinks occasionally and . . ."

Bridget had nodded with almost an approving smile. "Never mind . . . you are both handsome healthy young people. I'd be delighted to have him."

Christmas was wonderful. She had sent the children to Virginia a week earlier. And she and Barry had a week alone together. On Christmas Eve he gave her a small diamond circlet pin from Cartier's. She knew it only cost three hundred dollars. And she had spent fourteen hundred for the gold digital watch at

Tiffany's. He was like a child when he saw it. Then he said, "I wish I could have spent more for you . . . but I'm strapped. The few evenings I have to attend dinner parties means sending flowers . . . and I have to keep up the box at the opera . . . that wasn't included in the will . . . but Debbie and all of Constance's friends insist on it . . . and Jesus, I have to take one of them each time. It's not bad enough to be saddled with the opera, which I hate, but to be saddled with Debbie, and that sister of hers, Eleanora. She's almost as rich as Debbie and she's married to an AC-DC guy. You can imagine the thrilling evenings we all have together."

And then in March, Timothy Ryan died. Dolores had no choice but to spend the entire week with the family. It fell close to Easter so she took the children out of school and they went to the farm. The children enjoyed it immensely. Michael's children were there and Joyce was there with the new baby. Of course, Michael had various excuses to get back to New York, and some evenings he didn't make it back to the farm. Joyce was too preoccupied with the new baby to bother and Dolores found herself delegated as Bridget's companion. After Easter, Bridget pleaded with her to stay on—the other sisters had to return . . . their children went to parochial school . . . they had to get back. Dolores said her children had to get back also. Bridget sighed but made her promise to come every weekend. She held Dolores close. "I think I love you more than my own children. I understand you, Dolores. You know when my husband was young—and with five pregnancies almost in a row—he took up with a glamorous sculptress. She was mediocre in talent, but had the looks of a beauty queen. He kept her in grand style and bought exhibitions for her and forced his friends into buying her work. That liaison lasted ten years. Oh, he was always home on weekends, holidays . . . but I was left to raise the children. He even cheated on the sculptress with a refugee, a princess who had no money. He set her up very well and there's talk that the nephew who suddenly came to live with her a few years later is really his son. I know what you went through with Jimmy—like father, like son. I know that Michael's late evenings must be devoted to some woman, but Joyce is a placid girl—she's wrapped up in her children, it would never enter her mind that he would have another woman. And like me, she has the Church. But I feel for you— because even though you were born a Catholic, religion doesn't seem to play a large part in your life. Well, when I was newly married, all I had to turn to was the Church, and when one of my children was very ill with diphtheria, I prayed. And I promised I would go to Mass every day if she recovered. The doctors had given her up, but she started getting well the following day. And the Church has given me strength . . . turn to it, Dolores! Your children will grow up and leave you. Your body is filled with unfulfilled passion like mine was. But you'll find that in loving Jesus, our Lord . . . you will find a release and the inner strength will grow until it fills you. Oh, it won't be easy . . . but remember I'll always be here to help."

Dolores went back to New York. The children went to school. She called Barry's office and was informed he had gone to Bermuda over Easter. She relaxed . . . how could he know when she would return . . . he had called her when it had happened . . . he had come to the funeral . . . but she explained she had to stay on the farm over Easter.

She went to see a priest—one at the Paulist church who had always been kind and seemed more worldly than most. She explained how she did "believe" . . . and yet she didn't. He tried to counsel her. She went to confession. She said the Stations of the Cross, but she felt no inner strength. No . . . Bridget had found it, but maybe with Bridget it had always been there. If Jimmy hadn't been President, she would have walked out on him after he had his first affair. Timothy Ryan had not been President, yet Bridget had sat by and raised her children and turned to the Church for strength.

Life fell into its regular pattern. She

listened to Mary Lou's French lesson . . . helped her with the verbs . . . watched TV with the children . . . and at nine o'clock sent them off to bed. She was restless. At eleven o'clock she heard the slight ring of the door-bell announcing that the *News* and the *Times* had been dropped. She walked out and picked them up and carried them into her bedroom. She got into bed . . . suddenly her heart seemed to turn to lead. Barry's picture was on the front page of the *News*. In a quiet cere-mony in Bermuda, he had married Debbie Morrow!

She lay awake until three in the morn-ing. That made it eight in London. Then she placed the call to her sister. She got through immediately.

"Dolo." Nita was angry at being awak-ened. "What's the matter? I'm sorry I couldn't come for the funeral but we cabled flowers and all that."

"Forget the funeral. I want to ask you something."

"Couldn't you have waited until a civi-lized hour?"

"This can't wait. Find out if Baron Erick de Savonne still wants to marry me."

Nita was now wide awake. "You mean it!"

"Absolutely."

"Well, I'll track him down. I think he's in Paris . . . no . . . he was here last week

and was going to Switzerland. Let me find him
and I'll call you back."

Nita called back within an hour. "He
says Yes . . . and to lose twenty pounds . . .
he likes his women thin."

"When will I hear from him?"

"You're to cable him when you lose the
twenty pounds." Then Nita hung up.

31. A Happy Union

DOLORES went to a doctor Nita had told her about. She got the green pills that killed her appetite. She lived on black coffee . . . diet sodas . . and one meal of fish each day. She had the exercise man again and worked with him an hour each morning. She took sauna baths twice a week. At the end of five weeks she had lost twenty-two pounds. She called Nita. "I weigh one hundred and seven . . ."

"You can't . . . you're three inches taller than I . . . and I weigh one hundred and one."

"I weigh one hundred and seven. Tell him to come here and weigh me if he likes."

That afternoon twelve dozen roses arrived. The Baron arrived the following day at noon. He came directly to her apartment after calling her from the airport. She was wearing a pair of black slacks and a black sweater. She looked pencil-slim.

He stared at her when he entered and

nodded in agreement. "You have done a magnificent job. Now, about our wedding . . . I suggest it take place at my house in the country. It is eighteen miles from Paris, but it is like a castle. Your sister is already working on the guest list. I have invited all the dignitaries of state. Shall we break it to the newspapers here? My men are waiting."

"Before it breaks in the papers there is one thing you must do," she said quietly.

"What is that?"

"Come to Virginia with me and tell Bridget."

His smile was radiant. "It will be my pleasure. I have my plane waiting at your convenience at the airport."

"Let me call Bridget."

She went into the bedroom. Bridget answered immediately. "I was just about to have lunch. Are you feeling well?"

"Marvelous."

"Dolores, I don't want to sound like a nagging mother-in-law, but do you realize it's been over a month since you saw me."

"I've been attending to some important matters."

"You've gotten involved with the Church!"

"No, Bridget . . . I tried that. Look, this is urgent . . . may I come there and talk to you?"

"I was planning to surprise you and come to New York at the end of the week."

"This can't wait, Bridget. Can I fly down this afternoon?"

"Of course."

She returned to the living room. Erick was on the phone. He signaled her to be quiet, then he said, "Fine . . . buy it all up. I'll check with you later in the day." He hung up and turned to her. "Just a little business I had to attend to."

"I attended to mine," she said slowly. "My mother-in-law says we may come down this afternoon."

"Fine. We'll leave immediately. I'll tell the pilot." He went to the phone. She watched those heavy fingers on the dial. Those fingers would soon be touching her body . . . she would be expected to kiss those ugly thick lips. She dashed into the bedroom and quickly changed into a suit. But the skirt fell off her. Nothing fit her but a few pairs of pants. She put on the best pair and grabbed a jacket.

"I have no clothes," she said as she walked into the living room. "I'm so thin now, nothing fits."

"Tomorrow you will buy everything you need." They drove to the private airport in silence. She saw the plane waiting . . . the pilot and co-pilot standing at attention. A steward helped them in. Then Erick tossed a box at her. "Take off that coat. I brought you this one."

She opened the box and felt the un-believable softness of the sable. "Oh Erick . . . how beautiful . . . but I can't wear it over pants."

"You can do anything. Remember that. And I like you in those tight pants and tight sweaters. Put on the sable."

She tried it on and whirled through the plane like a child. The steward brought a huge tin of Iranian caviar and a bottle of champagne. "We break your diet today," Erick said. And like a child, Dolores sat in her sable and ate caviar all the way to Virginia.

Bridget showed no surprise when she saw Baron Erick de Savonne. She received him cordially. She acknowledged that they had met at her son's funeral.

"But this is a happy time. I have come to ask your daughter-in-law's hand in mar-riage."

Bridget stared at him for a moment. Then she looked at Dolores. "May I speak to my daughter-in-law alone?"

Erick bowed graciously and retreated to the living room. Dolores followed Bridget to a small den demurely.

"Take off that ostentatious coat," Brid-get said. "Sable in April!"

"He just gave it to me . . . on the plane."

"How long has this been going on?"

"He asked me to marry him a year ago
. . . when the children and I were visiting
Nita. I gave him an unqualified No."

"What caused you to change your
mind?"

"Bridget . . . I'm going to be forty
. . . there is no one . . . I can't make it each
year on the thirty thousand . . . I've been dig-
ging into my capital . . . borrowing from
Nita . . ."

"If you had told me I'd give you more."

"It's not that. My expenses will increase.
The twins will need to go to college. Mary
Lou will also go to college and have a proper
debut . . . I couldn't let you support me. Also,
the twins need a father."

"He's a grandfather!"

"Bridget." Dolores got on her knees and
put her head in the woman's lap. "I'm so lonely.
You're the only person I have. And you have
your own children and grandchildren. I have
no close friend. I'm tired of being a legend . . .
of pinching pennies . . . of using Michael as
an escort."

"What about the Supreme Court Justice?"

"What about him?" Dolores flared. "He's
past sixty and has no real money."

"Money," Bridget snorted. "Is that all
that matters to you?"

"Bridget, you've never been without it

. . . or had to worry about it—you can't understand. You've never had my kind of loneliness."

"But that man . . . couldn't there be someone else? Why didn't you encourage Barry Haines after his wife died? Now he was good-looking . . . the kind of a man you should have married."

"Bridget," Dolores said softly. "I loved him with all my heart. But he also had to marry for money. It almost broke my heart."

Bridget's eyes misted. "I had no idea . . . " Then she sighed. "Of course, you will have to break with the Church."

"I will raise my children as Catholics . . . but I will not be able to be married by a priest."

"Can you accept this?"

"Better than the loneliness and heartbreak I have known."

Bridget stood up and walked into the living room. She held out her hand to Erick. "Congratulations, sir . . . I hope you make my daughter-in-law happy."

He kissed her hand. "And would you honor us by coming to the wedding?"

"When and where will it be?"

"In my villa outside of Paris. In ten days. I will send my plane for you."

"I shall come . . . and so shall my son and my three daughters."

"Madame, you make me very proud," he said hoarsely.

"And now I must rest. I am not young, you know . . . and surprises take a great deal out of me. I shall also pray for your union to be a happy one."

32. The Bridal Suite

DOLORES couldn't believe the frenetic activity of the next ten days. She lost two more pounds and fought to keep the children from showing their sullenness toward Erick. The news made headlines all over the world. There were several meetings with lawyers for both sides as the marriage contracts were drawn up and signed. Then Erick whisked her and the children off to Paris and she was spared seeing the reams of publicity that berated her for this move. America was furious. Their Princess had deceived them. They had *made* her their Princess. And now she was theirs to vilify. Women wrote hate mail to newspapers. Editorials ran against the marriage . . . everyone seemed aghast at the merger . . . thousands and thousands of hate letters arrived addressed to her. After opening a few, she burst into tears. She was staying at the Ritz in Paris. Erick had taken a whole floor for her and the children and the servants he had gotten for her. He took her to every couturier. She knew he spent several hundred thousand on gowns, shoes, underwear, nightgowns. He bought her three more fur coats. And then the day before the wedding everyone went to his villa.

Bridget, Michael, Joyce, and the three sisters and their husbands had arrived. Erick had lavish suites for them. Dolores couldn't believe the "villa." It was like a castle. Her own "bridal suite" was a hundred-foot bedroom, a large dressing room, a room for shoes, another room for hats and a room for clothes and furs. Then there was another dressing room . . . a sauna . . . a bidet . . . and another room that had a sunken bathtub, large enough for six people to bathe in. There was an indoor swimming pool and ice-skating rink in the villa . . . there was an outdoor pool . . . and fifty acres of land that adjoined it.

The night before the wedding, Erick gave everyone gifts. Nita received a Vacheron diamond wristwatch. Bridget received an antique cross encrusted with gemstones. The children were given masses of games and toys and bicycles and a horse for each of them. Then Erick placed a huge ruby and diamond necklace around Dolores' neck and handed her earrings to match. "You put them on yourself." He waited while she put them on her ears . . .

then he took her hand and slid on the most
massive perfect diamond she had ever seen.

Everyone gasped. "How many carats
is it?" Nita asked.

"Sixty," Erick said. "It's the most perfect
gemstone in the world."

That night she slept in a guest suite. But
she was too excited to sleep. Never had she
seen money spent like this. She couldn't wait
until she saw their ocean liner. That afternoon
she had signed the final premarital contracts.
It was just as he had said it would be. She
wondered what would happen after the wedding. Maybe they'd go on a honeymoon on the
ocean liner . . . honeymoon . . . she ran her
hands down her slim body. Oh God . . . tomorrow night this body would be his . . . to
maul . . . to take. She could almost feel his
lips slobbering on her. She got out of bed and
swallowed two sleeping pills and washed them
down with some Scotch.

The maid had to rouse her the following
morning. She bathed in a lethargic state. The
hairdresser arrived. She was to stay in the suite
until five when the ceremony took place. Her
bridal gown was high-styled, demure . . .
perfect.

When she stood before the mirror she
realized she had never looked as beautiful. If
only Barry could see her . . . But he would,
because the Baron was going to allow the press

in after the wedding for a ten-minute interview
and photographic session. She wondered what
Barry thought of all this. Had he thought she'd
wait and eventually they'd go back to their old
arrangement? Well, she had shown him. She
had shown the world!

During the wedding ceremony, she had
not dared to look at Bridget or the children.
When it was over, she hugged everyone. A
lavish dinner was served. One hundred people
were seated. There was a butler behind every
second guest. There were gifts for all the
women.

At eleven o'clock the last guest had departed. She clung to Bridget. Erick was sending them all to Paris in his cars—he had
engaged suites for everyone at the Ritz. Tomorrow his private plane would take them
back to the States.

Dolores lay in bed in the bridal suite.
The house was empty. She was wearing her
white satin nightgown . . . she stared at the
empty bed beside her. When the last guest
had departed and they had gone to their bridal
chamber, she had watched him change into a
gray suit with amazement.

"Where are you going?"

"To my mistress . . . she is waiting."

And he had left her . . . untouched.
And he hadn't even tried to deceive her. It was
as cut and dried as that. She held out her hand

and stared at the ring. It glowed like fire in the semidarkness. She rubbed it against her satin nightgown . . . and stared at it as the tears ran down her cheeks. . . .